20 Greatest Explorers of the World

20 Greatest Explorers of The World

Kalyani Mookherji

Ocean Books Pvt. Ltd.
ISO 9001:2015 Publishers

Published by
Ocean Books (P) Ltd.
4/19 Asaf Ali Road,
New Delhi-110 002 (INDIA)
e-mail: info@oceanbooks.in

ISBN 978-81-8430-302-5
20 GREATEST EXPLORERS OF THE WORLD
by Kalyani Mookherji

Edition
2025

Price
₹ 300.00 (Rupees Three Hundred only)

Printed at
Narula Printers, Delhi

Author's Note

The urge to explore is an ancient one. While primitive humans were compelled to go beyond the limits of safety in search for food and shelter, later on the desire for resources and power through acquisition of such resources proved to be a determining factor in the history of human exploration. Riches like gold, precious commodities like spices and silk, land for colonization and human population for cheap labour or market have all figured as different motives for exploration at different periods in history. No less important has been the pure hunger for knowledge, just the desire to find out what lies beyond the horizon.

The book follows a chronological order in detailing the exploits of explorers, beginning with the famous Greek adventurers who were acting both as Geographers and Historians of their time in seeking out stranger shores, with a healthy dose of the mythological as well. The most impressive period of human exploration is of course the 15th-16th centuries which saw Europe engage in a determined effort to discover the rest of the world with the result that continents like North America, South America and Asia came to find a place in the newly-minted world maps. The 18th and 19th century explorers landed and came to know more about the continents of Africa and Oceania including, Australia and New Zealand. In 20th century, the last untrodden regions of the Earth like the North and South Poles, the highest point of the planet and lowest depths of the ocean became the target of modern explorers with the final frontier – the space – falling to human spirit of exploration in mid-20th century.

This book brings together only some of the names which have been credited with expanding the limits of the known world. Some of the names like Christopher, Columbus and Neil Armstrong are legendary and indeed can be found on the lips of any child. Then again some like Zheng He, the Chinese explorer of 15th century and Sacagawea, the Native American explorer of the western American frontier, are less famous, possibly because till now European male figures have garnered more attention than those belonging to other cultures and genders.

Another word on the frequent use of 'discovery', in the context of the landmark expeditions of the famous explorers. For instance, though Christopher Columbus has long been thought to be the first to discover the New World of the Americas, there were already Native American tribes living in those continents when Columbus's ship landed on the shores of West Indies. Even if this event is qualified as the discovery of American by a European, a Norseman named Leif Eriksson had already reached North America, nearly 500 years before Columbus did.

And yet these recent facts do not reduce the importance of Columbus's expeditions in any way. Instead what continuing research brings up is the dynamic nature of human exploration. No particular expedition or finding or information is set in stone – each venture takes its strength from those who have already travelled before and in turn, leaves a legacy for future explorers to push the limits of the known world still farther.

Contents

1

Herodotus

(484 BCE-C424 BCE)

Humans have been exploring ever since the first evolution of the species when it was imperative to go far and wide in search of food or safe shelter. Eventually, the earliest human societies may have migrated vast distances to explore richer resources which would ensure better survival of their community.

However, the proper history of human exploration can be said to have begun with the ancient Greeks, since they were one of the earliest to document their expeditions and thus provide a reference point to scholars of the later centuries, at least in the European world. And among the explorers of classical Greece, one name stands tall – Herodotus of Halicarnassus.

Father of History

Today, Herodotus is primarily known as the person who carved out the field of study which the modern world knows as 'history'. Cicero, the famous writer and orator of classical Rome in fact hailed Herodotus as, 'The Father of History'. This accolade was mainly based on Herodotus' famous work, *The Histories* which was published in 415 BC. The exhaustive book is divided in nine chapters, each being dedicated to one of the Muses who in Greek Mythology are the goddesses of the various arts such as music, dance and poetry and who were believed to inspire artists to reach ever greater creative and intellectual heights. The First Chapter is presided over by Clio, the Muse of History after which the book goes on to describe the exploits of four Persian kings. The first of them is Cyrus after which Herodotus deals with the events in the reign of Cambyses. The reign of the Persian King Darius takes up the largest chunk of the world and continues till Chapter 6. Finally, the exploits of the Persian King Xerxes are dealt with in the Chapters 7 and 8, which in effect rounds off *The Histories.*

In all, *The Histories* provides a fascinating account of the Greek scholar's travels through Greece, Egypt, Asia Minor, accounts of important historical events like the 'Battles of Marathon and Peluseum' as well as descriptions of The Seven Wonders of the Ancient World.

This was a time when the division between various fields of knowledge was not as clearly marked as in modern times. A single scholar was often an expert in writing narratives of historical events, travelling to new places, enunciating philosophical theories, dealing with matters of state and even perhaps fighting in wars. Thus, the roles of historian, philosopher, statesman, fighter and explorer often merged and this was what happened in the case of Herodotus too.

Life of Herodotus

In the Prologue to his *The Histories*, Herodotus mentions that he is a native of Halicarnassus which lies on the south-west coast of Asia Minor, in modern-day Turkey. Little else is clear about his life but it seems fairly certain that he hailed from a prosperous family, since he was not only able to fund his own education but the high quality of his writings in *The Histories* suggests that he had studied in one of the best schools of the day. This view is also based on his proficiency in Ionian dialect of Greek, knowledge of which was available to select students during those times.

Also Herodotus' ability to travel for leisure and at will suggests that he had recourse to private income and was not dependent on any employer. During his travels, he might have at some point served in the army, since his accounts of wars are quite accurate and mostly from the perspective of a foot soldier.

Eventually, Herodotus is thought to have settled down in the

Italian island of Thurii which was a Greek colony at the time, though there are some historical accounts that he may have returned to Athens as well. During the course of his life, Herodotus seems to have an uneasy relationship with his birthplace. Evidence from an 11th-century Byzantine lexicon, the *Suda*, suggests that he was at some point banished from Halicarnassus by the ruler Lygdamis and had to leave for the island of Samos. He returned to his place of birth to support the rebellion against Lygdamis but again fell afoul of the populace because of which he was forced to leave for Thurii.

Herodotus died sometime between 425 and 413 BCE, probably because of the plague in Athens. Interestingly more than one city, Athens and Thurii among them, claimed to be the last resting place of the famous historian and constructed memorials in his honour – yet another example of the vast popularity and influence that Herodotus commanded in his day.

Herodotus as Explorer

As an explorer, Herodotus is mainly remembered for his remarkable tales of travels through Egypt, down into Africa and further east in Asia Minor. His book mentions his travels to well-known places like Babylon, Thrace, Scythia, Colchis, the Persian capital city of Susa as well as through the islands of Archipelago. He seems to have not only touched the shores of Black Sea, going till as far as the Dnieper but his mention of Gaza implies that he knew about Palestine as well.

The enthusiastic tales of his travels have exposed Herodotus to disbelief, both during his own times and later on as well. In his, *The Histories*, he talks of 'The Seven Wonders of the World' and while describing Babylon, he lavishes praise on the vast size of the city as well as hundred gates set in the wall bordering the city. Modern archaeology has come to the conclusion that Babylon's territorial dimensions were much more modest than claimed by Herodotus and the city had around eight gates instead of the hundred as appears in the writings of Herodotus. Similar accounts of other ancient cities and cultures in Africa and Asia Minor appear to be too fantastic to be true and later scholars have pointed out that many are widely diverging from facts – in fact some historians even believe that the only travel Herodotus did was in his mind and all the descriptions of his explorations through new lands and cultures are largely the figment of his imagination.

It is only recently that modern wildlife and ethnographic expeditions have found some kernel of truth in what has been largely seen as Herodotus' tall stories. One chapter in *The Histories* mentions his travels through West Asia where he claims to have come across accounts of ants the size of foxes and which, incredibly, when digging their mounds throw up gold sand. For long such accounts have been regarded as fabulous and catering to a gullible reading audience, hungry for fantasies of man and beast in different cultures. It was only recently in 1984 that French scientist Michel Pessler noted that a fox-shaped marmot indeed existed in the Himalayas where certain slopes containing gold nuggets may have been dug up by these creatures, thus giving the appearance of gold-digging animals to the local populace who lived nearby.

Also Pessler remarked that the local word for the marmot was very similar to what translated as, "mountain ant" and Herodotus may have confused the two with the result that he thought the creature was a giant size ant when what he was actually describing was a type of marmot. So though Herodotus may have indulged in a little embroidery of facts – in keeping with the demands of contemporary audiences – modern research is showing that his major discoveries may not have been quite so far off the mark.

Yet, another aspect that the apparently fantastic tales of Herodotus need to be considered from is that of literary conventions. In those times, writers primarily plied their craft to come up with works that could be narrated in a public space, like Homer's *Iliad*, and not silently read in the isolation of a library. This oral context may have influenced Herodotus to embroider his book, *The Histories* with some elements of fantasy and exaggeration so that his audiences could be regaled. It was not until 415 BC, towards the end of his life, that *The Histories* was published in the prose form and till then it can be safely assumed that its popularity was largely due to efficiency as oral performance pieces.

Though the accounts of his travels and important historic events are not always strictly accurate, what these writings lose out on authenticity often make up in impact. Herodotus is able to put his reader right in the midst of the events of *The Histories* by creating vivid scenes with interesting characters and, sometimes, even dialogue. In fact, one of the main reasons why *The Histories* of Herodotus became popular in his time was because of their entertaining nature which may not have pleased the severest critics but ensured the lasting appeal of the books and in the process the survival of these documents down the centuries. It is quite likely that because of their popularity, *The Histories* have lived to tell the tale of contemporary travels and historical events, and had they been arid realistic versions, they may have been lost to obscurity.

The Histories in Context

In weaving the elements of history, geography, mythology and the fantastic, Herodotus was largely following the conventions of his time. History as the objective retelling of important events of the past was not yet known and writers often merged various elements as well as their own subjective attitudes into such accounts. The same probably was true of Herodotus as well. Thus, it is likely that because both the Thebans and Corinthians refused to offer him patronage, they come out quite negatively in his works whereas since Athens granted him ample funds for his travels and writing, the city-state and its events are represented more positive in *The Histories*. Even in the account of his travels, Herodotus was rarely an impartial observer; in fact, the descriptions of new places, people, cultures and customs are mingled with lengthy strains of his personal opinions and what he thought of all that he saw. In the end, no matter what the level of authenticity he maintains, this is much beyond doubt that Herodotus did more than other writers of his day to document the events of the immediate past and his day in a structured form which in turn is the only one to have survived in the form of *The Histories*.

No account of Histories can be complete without putting it in context to Homer's *Iliad* to which it partly aspires and from which it partly turns away. That Herodotus was largely inspired by the Iliad and looked upon Homer with admiration is not in doubt, since he structures the larger arrangement of his *The Histories* on Homer's form in epics like *Iliad*. Similarly, the passage on Babylon in *The Histories* bears many resemblances to Homer's description of Egyptian Thebes in the epics. And yet Herodotus was no mere emulator of the master's literary style and narrative and in fact questioned the historical veracity of *The Iliad*, pointing out that it is highly improbable that the Achaeans would wage such a lengthy and costly campaign as the Trojan War just to get back a woman.

Even more importantly, Herodotus differed from Homer on the basic premise of his work. While the great epic writers like Homer before him and Virgil later on followed the literary convention of calling upon the gods to offer divine inspiration for their works, Herodotus did not feel the need to seek any divine assistance of this kind. He was quite clear that *The Histories* was the result of his own efforts and gleaned from his own travels.

Histories and their Significance in Exploration

Though today *The Histories* of Herodotus is largely credited as the first attempt at documenting historical events in the ancient world, their importance in the history of human exploration is no less significant. Herodotus' qualification in the first chapter of his *The Histories* that the book is about the exploits of man and not necessarily about the feats of gods and their human subjects is a trailblazer in itself. The root word of history is the Greek *historia* which was originally used to describe investigation and inquiry. In keeping with this original meaning, Herodotus' *The Histories* are an attempt to inquire upon human achievements by travelling far beyond the limits of his country, sometimes by witnessing new people, lands and cultures himself and sometimes by recounting of what he heard from others, Herodotus exemplified the spirit of both the historian and the explorer. His *The Histories* are thus not only a documentation of historical events like wars and battles but also of new places and in this way, he stands out as one of the earliest explorers of the world.

Finally, Herodotus and his works give people of his times an awareness of their place in the world. By recounting the main historical events of the times as well as by describing the far-off places, he is able to help his fellow-men, and perhaps even people of future times, appreciate the diversity and richness of the world that they inhabit and seek to take the search further.

□

2

Pytheas

(C. 380 BC-C. 300 BCE)

For most of the part of ancient culture, the notion of an explorer did not exist in isolation. Someone like Herodotus who went on travels through unknown places would have also been a historian, narrator, soldier and maybe philosopher and statesman. It is because of this that Pytheas becomes an important figure because according to many chroniclers of human exploration, the Greek was the first explorer in the modern sense of the term – in other words, a figure who set out specifically to find out unknown parts of the world, whether for economic or philosophical reasons.

Life and Times of Pytheas

Pytheas was born roughly around 380 BC in a place called Massalia which today would be known as Marseilles, in the southern coast of France. At the time of Pytheas's birth, Massalia was a Greek colony.

Till the time of the ancient Greeks, the Egyptians and earliest travellers had not really ventured far into the seas; they tended to stay close to the land and use coastal reference to guide their ships and boats, following a navigational technique known as piloting. However, with the flowering of classical Greek science and knowledge, there came about great advancements in knowledge of seafaring too. Using mathematical principles, Greek explorers learned to use the sun, constellations, the North Star and even sea conditions to help chart their course over open water. They were also the first to develop sophisticated models and maps which provided a major fillip to their nautical expeditions. All this brought about a heightened understanding of the ocean and the earth. For example, many centuries before Magellan circumnavigated the globe, the Greeks knew that the earth was a sphere and not a flat plane as was the accepted theory of earth during the Middle Ages. Pytheas gained a tremendous lot from the best of Greek mathematics and navigational science and grew up to be an astronomer, geographer and navigator.

Pytheas and the Tin Trade

Despite his education, Pytheas was not very rich, as evident from the accounts of Polybius, a Greek writer from a century after Pytheas. This means that Pytheas would have had to depend upon a wealthy Greek merchant to finance his expeditions. It is quite likely that his patron was associated with the trade of the metal tin which was known as "Kassiteros" in Greek. At the time, tin was a highly sought-after metal since when combined with copper, it was used to produce a very strong, tensile and malleable alloy, bronze which had several uses, ranging from the manufacture of coins and ornaments to that of tools and weapons. In fact, weapons made of bronze were particularly favoured by the Greek armies of the time because the alloy made the weapons both strong and lightweight.

Though tin was highly prized by the traders in Greek colonies and most of Europe, the major part of the tin trade was controlled by the Carthaginians. Then known as the Kassiterides Islands, the British Isles were well known to the Phoenicians as a principal source of tin. Even the Greek historian Herodotus had written about the source of the metal which could be reached by sailing through Pillars of Hercules – now known as the straits of Gibraltar – then north along the coast of Gaut to an area roughly equivalent to modern-day Cornwall in England. But the Greek traders had limited access to the metal since the Pillars of Hercules that marked the exit from the Mediterranean into the Atlantic, were in the control of the Carthaginians. In order to get past the Carthaginians, Pytheas may have either travelled on foot to cross the land till or more likely sailed, slowly and carefully, from his native Massalia to the Pillars of Hercules before turning north to the Kassiterides Isles. Choosing a time when the Carthaginians were busy in conflict – like their war with Syracuse in Sicily between 310-306 BC – may also have helped Pytheas to escape the notice of Carthaginians.

Voyage of Pytheas

The voyage of Pytheas detailing his journey from Brittany to mineral-rich Cornwall as well as the circumnavigation of the British Isles is supposed to have been documented in his major work, *On the Ocean.* But since this is now lost, most of the knowledge about his expeditions is gleaned from the writings of the Greek historian Polybius (*c.* 200–*c.* 118 BC) as well as others like Pliny and Pindar.

Though Pytheas apparently set off from his native port in search of an alternative route to the islands which were a source of tin, to a great extent, he must have been inspired by the pure thrill of adventure, the sheer delight of discovering new lands and sailing through unchartered oceans. Roughly around 330 BC, Pytheas reached the Port of Corbilo at the mouth of the Loire river. From there, he sailed to the island of Ouessant off the tip of Brittany. His main destination was Belerium also known as land's end in Cornwall, the main source of tin and which lay at the south-western tip of Britain. Along the way, he stopped and travelled for short distances inland and described the customs of the inhabitants. Apparently, he was as much impressed by the hospitality of the people who lived around the headland of Belerium as he was by the process of extraction of tin that the locals had developed over the years.

From Cornwall, Pytheas sailed north over the Irish sea. Going past between Britain and Ireland, he travelled all the way to the northern tip of Scotland and perhaps he may have gone as far out as the Orkney Islands. During the course of this journey, Pytheas was often amazed by the ways and practices of people living in this part of the world. The keen observer and writer that he was,

Pytheas diligently noted down events and anecdotes that were new and strange to him. One such account was related to him by some inhabitants of northern Scotland who described a place even further north were during certain times of the year, there were only two or three hours of night. Even more incredible was the story of places still north, where the sun could be seen shining at all times, without there being any 'night'. Though at the times, such accounts seemed fantastic to the travellers from the Mediterranean region, today people know that they were the first accounts of the phenomenon of Midnight Sun witnessed in lands lying close to the Arctic Circle.

Just like he was interested in geographical discoveries, Pytheas also painstakingly noted down the different ways and practices of the people living in these northern islands. He was told of people living in houses made of log and clay who because of severe cold climate stored their grains underground. This was nothing short of incredible to these travellers from warmer Mediterranean regions just as they were surprised to find that here grains were threshed in covered structures instead of in the mist of open fields.

Island of Thule

From the northern parts of Scotland, Pytheas set sail still further north and on the way saw a kind fish – the whale – he had never encountered before. In his accounts, Pytheas mentions passing a cluster of small islands where the crew notice large, boat-size fish, lazily swimming on the surface and loudly blowing out sprays of water. Though such pods of whales are common to these northern waters, to Pytheas and his Mediterranean crew, the sight of such sea creatures must have been indeed amazing.

Next, Pytheas mentions sailing northwards for six days and then reaching the land of Thule, which probably means contemporary Norway, though some historians believe may even have meant Iceland or Greenland. Another name that Pytheas gives to this region is Hyperborea; since Boreas to the Greeks referred to the God of the north wind, thus any land further northward was the land of Hyperboreans. Here the inhabitants lived on wild berries and "millet" – which here probably means oats and made a drink from wild honey which likely refers to mead. Pytheas described them as a people who are healthy and happy-go-lucky in nature – apparently no disease or suffering ails them and they often hold feasts and celebrations as an indication of their positive attitude to life. While to the modern reader, this seems something of an exaggeration, far more identifiable are Pytheas's descriptions of the icy, foggy weather that he often encountered in his journey along these islands. He writes of fog so dense and the waters so choked with icy slush that it was impossible for man or boat to cross them and travel further.

Though reports of a sea turned solid with ice may have been incredible to people back home, it was probably because of such foggy and icy conditions that Pytheas was forced to turn back from the "Land of Thule". Historians are still at odds over whether Pytheas actually visited places so near the Arctic Circle or simply reported anecdotes that he heard from people of the northern islands that he really visited. No matter what was the northernmost limit of his travel, his influence remains in the way the northern lands are now symbolically referred to as Thule – Greenland in fact has an actually place named Thule which also serves as the northernmost Air Base for the United States Air Force.

Journey Back Home

From Thule, Pytheas turned back for Britain and sailed down its east coast, crossing the north sea to the north Frisian islands off the coast of Germany till he reached the island of Helgoland, which he called Abalus. One of the most significant descriptions about this place is about amber, which he reported not only as being used by the local inhabitants as fuel but also constituting an important item of trade. Since this region was the richest source of amber in Europe, it is likely that Pytheas may have visited the Germanic coast of the Baltic Sea, thus also becoming the first explorer from the ancient Greek civilization to have come upon the Baltic region and the Germanic cultures.

From Abalus, Pytheas turned back at the mouth of the Vistula where it borders Scythia. He then sailed back along the coast of Europe and returned home to the port of Massalia.

After his return, Pytheas was upset to find that people did not believe his accounts of the geography and people in the northern lands – tales of midnight sun, seas with drifting ice as well as lands where people threshed grains indoors seemed far too unbelievable to his countrymen. This was partly due to the accepted theory of the time that the waters were frozen a lot further south than in reality, so it was not possible for boats to sail through the northern oceans. Even Pytheas's book was lost and eventually his journey came to exist only in the writings of other historians who quoted him when narrating their stories.

Other Achievements of Pytheas

Pytheas was the first to associate the tides to the phases of the moon. And even though his measurements of tides may not have been completely accurate, he could predict tides in the Atlantic based on the phases of the moon while exploring the Mediterranean and the Atlantic. Also by virtue of describing the foggy and ice-filled slushy waters that he encountered on his journey to the northern islands, he may actually have been the first European to discover the ocean, in this case, the Arctic Ocean. This is because the earliest Egyptians and other seafaring travellers tended to stay close to the shore, using coastal references to navigate. But Pytheas was probably the first to venture much further out from the seas and well into the major oceans.

In all these great discoveries, Pytheas was helped by his sturdy training as a mathematician and astronomer. This training helped him to inculcate the habits of observing and recording his findings on his voyages which in turn proved valuable to his navigational skills. In fact, in this role, he became quite adept at the use of the "gnomon", an instrument similar to the sextant used by Greek and Phoenician sailors since the 6th century BC with it, a skilled navigator would be able to find the way about even away from the sight of land and to perform highly complex calculations too about the ship's position on the seas.

Even more importantly, his background as a mathematician helped him to calculate latitudes. Pytheas is in fact one of the first persons who used the "gnomon" to calculate the latitude of a place. He used it to determine the latitude of his native town Massalia, which he found to be 43° 11' north, almost matching the correct figure of 43° 18' north for modern-day Marseilles.

Finally, Pytheas also discovered a way to determine location in relation to how far north or south one was from the north star. To do this, he measured the angle between the horizon and the north star. All this discoveries were to have a major impact on the science of open-ocean navigation. With the ability to record the precise location of different sites, he could navigate his ships' path through the open oceans with far more accuracy than before. However, what is even more important in the context of his legacy is that his mathematical and navigation techniques have helped to provide the proof needed for modern-day historians to confirm the course of his journeys and exploration.

The Legacy of Pytheas

Pytheas is now considered as the first explorer in the modern sense of word. He not only set out on his expeditions based on the express purpose of finding new lands and sea-routes – rather than accompanying an army or narrating a story – but used the most advanced mathematical and navigational techniques of the day in his endeavours. At the same time, Pytheas was not just a sea-navigator but a true explorer at heart who held a healthy curiosity about the practices and cultures of people he encountered on his journeys. He stopped at many points along the way to explore the area – sometimes he would simply refresh the boat's water and provisions but at other times he would travel inland with his crew. During such journeys, he would carefully record the geographical features of the place as well as the visible or reported practices and appearances of the inhabitants in such detail that the great British explorer, Sir Clement Markham reportedly declared that Pytheas was, indeed, the discoverer of Great Britain.

□

3

Leif Eriksson

(C. 970-1020)

The notion that Earth was a round globe rather than a flat surface was known to the Ancient Greeks among whom explorers like Pytheas (C. 380 BC – C. 330 BC) set out to discover the lands that lay far north and near the Arctic Circle. However, the adverse weather conditions and navigational difficulties put a halt to any more explorations to the west. It would be at least another thousand years that a Viking named Leif Eriksson would not only push the north-western limits of the known world but possibly became the first European to set foot in the New World.

Early Life

Born in Iceland sometime around 970 AD, Leif Eriksson was the son of Erik the Red. In keeping with the Viking traditions, when Leif attained boyhood, he was sent away from his family to live and learn the ways of his community. At about eight years of age, a man named Thyrker – whom Erik the Red had brought from Germany – was given the responsibility of teaching Erik about Viking customs and livelihood. Under the keen eye of Thyrker, Erik learnt to speak the Celtic and Russian languages as well as write and read runes, besides listening to ancient tales of Norse gods, goddesses and heroes. More importantly, Thyrker taught Erik the Viking techniques of warfare and the use of weapons. An important part of these growing up years was the love of seafaring and nautical adventures that young Leif developed, not only as a result of all the Old Norse mythological stories but also because of the sailors and their lore that Leif came to listen to during his apprenticeship at Thyrker's house.

When young Leif turned twelve, he was ordered to return to his father's house and very soon a dramatic incident took place which changed the course of Leif's life and brought him nearer to his destiny. The spring after Leif's return, his father Erik was asked to attend the Thingvellior or an assembly of leaders which made laws for the Viking community. There Erik got into a fight with a long-time enemy and soon things escalated to a point where Erik was accused of murder and banished from the community. As a result, Leif along with other family members, slaves and limited provisions accompanied his father as the latter set sail to find the lands rumoured to lie to the west of Iceland. Since Erik was in trouble with authorities in Norway too, he steered his journey further towards the west in search of a land where he could settle and live in peace. This voyage from Iceland on the western waters marked the first time young Leif was been exposed to deep-sea sailing and found that his boyhood desires of sailing into the open ocean had come true in the most unexpected way.

Arrival in Greenland

Banished from Iceland for three years, Erik sailed westwards till he arrived on the shores of Greenland. While the land seemed inhospitable at first, eventually, Erik and his dependents settled down to a quiet but fruitful way of life. For young Leif, this time was again one of learning and adapting to new geographical conditions, a lesson that would come in very useful in his future expeditions.

Once Erik's stipulated of banishment was over, he decided to go make a trip back to Iceland and when there, he told people all about the new life in Greenland. Because economic conditions had been steadily worsening in Iceland – famines and overgrazing had resulted in loss of vegetation cover and food – many people listened to Erik's accounts with interest and decided to follow Erik to Greenland.

Leif in the meantime was on the doorstep of manhood and his potential for bravery and adventure was increasing becoming evident. One such incident that gave indication of great promise was when Leif managed to capture a live polar bear, all by himself. From the shore, Leif saw the huge animal standing on the ice flow but the presence of a strong current between the ice flow and land made any attempt at venturing out into the waters rather dangerous. Leif however brought to use his inherent knowledge of the sea currents, sailed upstream from the polar bear and then while allowing his boat to be guided by the current into the ice-flow, managed to get his prey. This incident not only impressed men much older to him in his community but marked him out for great things to come.

Destiny soon came calling. One day Leif spotted an old, weather-beaten boat sailing very slowly into the harbour. When Leif enquired about it, he realized that the boat belonged to the expedition of the renowned sea Captain Bjarni Hergelfson who had set sail for the lands on the western waters more than a year back. Leif was now determined to make Bjarni's acquaintance to learn all about the mysterious lands that lay to the west of Greenland. Bjarni's recounted how the crew had been facing navigational problems because of the cloud cover that diminished the possibility of finding their way about on the seas with the help of the North Star. Even then the crew kept on sailing and finally reached a shore which unlike Greenland was not covered with ice but green, flat and forested. However, there was no time to get ashore and explore the new land since Bjarni's expedition was already behind schedule and he wanted to get to Greenland as quickly as possible. The account of this voyage had a powerful impact on Leif who was now convinced that a rich, fertile land lay much west of Greenland and the discovery would be beneficial if only he could find a way to reach it.

The First Voyage

With all these thoughts of expeditions germinating in his mind, Leif grew increasingly restless to embark on a voyage all on his own. At around twenty-four years of age, Leif's wish was granted and he was allowed to captain a ship with a crew of fourteen members but which would also be guided by Thyrker's long seafaring knowledge and experience. The immediate purpose of the voyage was to take gifts to the ruler of Norway, King Olaf; however in the heart of his hearts, Leif ardently wished that he in the course of his journey would be able to find out something about the unknown lands that lay to the west.

At the beginning, the voyage was helped by favourable winds but after two days, the winds dropped down to only a slight breeze which meant that Leif's boats could not sail as fast as he would have liked them to. While a nautical journey to Iceland would have taken only two days under the usual circumstances, this time it took Leif's boat around five days to touch the shore of Iceland.

In order to make up for lost time, Leif forbade his crew to go ashore which is why there was no restocking of provisions. Leif would eventually go on to fret over this decision since after leaving the vicinity of Iceland, the expedition seemed to lose its way and continued to sail for many days. In the end, just when Leif thought the ship would run out of food, he received news that land was in sight. However, this was not the destination Leif had been sailing towards and when he found that he had come upon the Hebrides Islands, he realized that the ship had travelled much more towards south than would have been necessary to reach Norway.

After Leif's arrival upon the Hebrides Islands, a long and fierce storm swept over the place. There was no question of setting sail then and Leif found himself as well as his crew stuck on the island for around a month as the storm raged on. According to some historical anecdotes, during this time, Leif was met by a young woman named Thorgunna who was the daughter of the chief of the islands. Believed to be well-versed in the magical arts, Thorgunna apparently predicted that she would have a son by Leif who would be named Thorgils. Years later Thorgils would visit Leif in Greenland and receive recognition as his son. Though more details are hard to come by, Thorgils seems to be the only offspring of Leif that exists in historical anecdotes.

Leif in Norway

After the storm passed on, Leif and his crew were able to set sail from the Hebrides Islands. This time they were amply aided by favourable winds and they were able to arrive at the shores of Norway without delay. In the royal court of Norway, Leif was greeted with great cordiality by King Olaf Tryggvason who not only remarked that he knew Leif's father well but also agreed to hear Leif's adventures with great interest.

After Leif finished the account of his voyages, the king was highly pleased with the young man's bravery and courage and he strongly exhorted Leif to spend some time at the court. The kingdom of Norway was then a place of affluence and at the royal court, Leif found himself partaking of every kind of luxury.

One day however during a game of chess between King Olaf and Leif, the discussion turned to more serious subjects. The king told Leif that though earlier he too had worshipped Norse gods and goddesses, now he was a follower of Christianity. Apparently, the king had converted in the wake of a disastrous plague that left thousands of people in his country dead. Once the king along with other countrymen was baptized, the plague disappeared and since then the king has been an ardent believer in Christianity.

Leif became curious about this new religion and allowed himself to be baptized as well. It is believed that soon after he returned to Greenland and even brought back a priest who would spread the new faith in the country.

Leif's Voyage to the New World

Though Leif had returned to Greenland to much fame and recognition, deep inside he still felt that he had not really achieved all that he was meant to do. Bjarni's accounts of a new land with lush green forests and flat terrain kept echoing in his mind until he decided to set off on a new voyage in search of this mysterious land in the far west. For this Leif purchased Bjarni's boat and then assembled a small but qualified crew which again included the much knowledgeable and experienced Thyrker. Leif decided to follow Bjarni's course as far as possible; thus after keeping to the western coast of Greenland, he sailed further west for around 600 miles and eventually came up to a land marked by high mountains of ice and rock.

Leif named this place Helluland which translates as Flat Rock Land or Slab Land and perhaps corresponds to modern-day Baffin Island. The arrival of the boat on this barren land with only rocks of ice was something of a disappointment to both Leif and his crew since they had been hoping to arrive upon a more pleasant coast with vegetation and good weather.

Disappointed but not daunted, Leif continued to sail southwards and eventually arrived at a coast with white beaches and few trees. He named this place Markland which is now believed to be the modern-day equivalent of eastern coast of Canada. From this point, Leif continued to sail in a south-easterly direction and eventually arrived at a most fertile-looking place. This was an island with a mainland behind it – here the grass smelled sweet and fresh while waters off the island was teeming with salmon far bigger than the crew had ever seen before. Also there were green fields ideal as pastureland for their cattle while the forests beyond proved to be rich sources of timber, fruit and other necessities.

Leif initially had plans to build just a few small and temporary shelters to house the crew while they scoped out the land. But tempted by the richness of resources here, Leif ordered the building of a large house which would shelter them till after the winters. In the course of the explorations, one day Thyrker returned with the news that he had found grapes growing wild; the news created great excitement among the new settlers and they were even more thankful for the bounties of the land.

Leif next ordered his men to stock as much of the fruits and timber on the boat as was possible so that they may have enough to eat through the winter. However, when the cold season came, Leif and his crew were amazed to find that they were not to be snowed in or cut off by icy sleet. There was no frost to damage plants nor endless days of fog and darkness. The experience of this milder winter was an entirely new thing for the crew who were used to harsh, icy, dark and lengthy winters. Because of the fertile and pleasing nature of the land, Leif named this place Vin Land – after the grapes which were discovered growing wild here – which historians believe corresponds to modern-day L'Anseaux Meadows in the Newfoundland province of Canada. In the early 1960s, archaeological excavations turned up evidence of what is generally believed to be the base camp of the 11th-century Viking exploration.

Leif's Legacy

Curiously, despite coming upon such a bountiful land off the eastern coast of Canada, Leif and his crew did not settle down permanently. With the arrival of the warm season, they left for their home in Greenland again. It is believed that only Leif's brother Thorvald and a handful of would-be settlers returned to the Canadian coast but even they were killed by the Indian tribes soon after their arrival. Leif himself spent the last days of life promoting Christianity. Though his father proved unreceptive to the Christian faith, Leif was able to convert his mother, Thjodhild, who had Greenland's first Christian church built at Brattahild. When Erik the Red died, Leif Eriksson took over as Chief of the Greenland settlement. Though Thorgill, Leif's son by Thorgunna was accepted by Leif, the young man could never be popular in the community and could not aspire to follow in his father's footsteps. After Leif's death in 1025, the chiefdom apparently passed on to another son Thorkel Leifsson, after which nothing more is known about Leif's descendents.

The only references to this great Scandinavian explorer remained buried in the old Norse sagas which have always narrated the feats of Viking gods and heroes. One of these was the Icelandic saga, the Groenlendinga saga or, "Saga of the Greenlanders", and another was the 13th-century Icelandic Eiriks saga or, "Saga of Erik the Red", which eulogized the victories of Erik the Red and his sons, including Leif Eriksson.

No wonder then that for a long time, the majority of the world remained oblivious to the fact that Leif Eriksson had been among the first people from Europe to arrive upon the Canadian coast, nearly five centuries before Christopher Columbus would arrive in 1492. It was only in the 20th century that the world started paying true homage to the Norse explorer, an example of which was the announcement of US President Calvin Coolidge in 1925, at the 100th anniversary celebrations of the arrival of the first official group of Norwegian immigrants in the United States, that that Eriksson had indeed been the first European to discover America.

□

4

Marco Polo

(C. 1254-1324)

The notion of humans exploring the world has always existed on many levels – at its most obvious it signifies geographical discoveries like those of continents and islands but on another level, it is also about sailing through unchartered territories of the imagination – taking facts and travels and reinventing them in such a way so as to impress and inspire people in different times and places. This was the kind of adventure that Venetian traveller and writer Marco Polo engaged in and for what he is remembered today – as one of the most influential if not the most truthful explorers of human history.

The Times

In the 13th and 14th centuries, the lands of the Far East were an object of great mystery and fascination to the people in Europe. Traders returned from those lands not only with rare and luxurious products like silk and gems but also brought back tales of fabulous wealth and beauty, strange people and society in those parts of Asia. China especially was a highly exotic idea in the mind of the Europeans – for one it was the source of many precious and useful objects but most of all, its inaccessibility made it fascinating. High mountains, vast deserts and treacherous oceans made it difficult to reach and hence inflamed the desire to learn even more about it.

At the time of Marco Polo's journey, the most powerful king in China was Kublai Khan. He was a descendent of Mongol kings who were known for their fierce horseback warfare and on the strength of which they had come down from Central Asia to conquer vast parts of China. Though Kublai Khan's father Genghis Khan was also a Mongol, he also understood the finer points of statesmanship and governance. Thus, he and later Kublai Khan were open to learning about the military, politics and ways of different cultures which is why foreign travellers, merchants, craftsmen and diplomats were accorded a warm welcome in the Great Khan's court. For the same reason, emperor was keen on having missionaries as well as well-educated guests from European countries and this is how Marco Polo came to find a place of honour in Kublai Khan's court.

One of the few sources of information about the fantastic land of the East was the merchants who regularly travelled on the Silk Road. This was a series of trade routes from Central Asia to Europe and was then the only means of contact with the people of the Far East. Marco Polo himself travelled many times along the Silk Road and other ancient trade routes leading to countries of Central Asia and all that he saw and learnt during his journeys was compiled into a book titled, *The Description of the World*, or more simply, *The Travels of Marco Polo*. This was one of the first sources of information about China and other Asian lands written for popular reading in Europe and its impact on later explorers was tremendous.

Early Life of Marco Polo

Born in Venice in 1254, Marco Polo was mainly brought up by his mother and rarely saw his father at home during his childhood years. This was because his father, Nicolo Polo, was a successful trader and often away on journeys. By early 13th century tales of fabulous wealth in the lands of East had started doing the rounds in commercial centres of Europe like Venice and in 1260, Nicolo with his brother Matteo decided to head for this promising land. In 1265, the brothers found their way to Kaifeng which was then the capital city of the empire led by the powerful Mongol ruler, Kublai Khan. After a stay of four years, the Polo brothers set off for their homeland, but with an unusual request from the Great Khan – that the Pope send holy oil as well as a hundred Christian missionaries to the Mongol kingdom, apparently to spread the word of Christ. Though the holy oil blessed by the Pope was not very difficult to obtain, the Pope did not pay any serious attention to the request of the missionaries; only two Friars initially agreed to the mission of travelling to China, but later even they opted out after only a short way into the journey.

In the Polo family, things had been changing – Nicolo's wife had passed away leaving behind their fifteen year old son Marco. This time Nicolo decided to take Marco along on his travels and soon enough in 1271, the Polo brothers together with a young, eager Marco set off again on the road to the East.

Macro Polo's First Journey to China

During the course of their journey from Venice to China, the Polo brothers together with young Marco decided to follow the trade routes passing through countries such as Persia and India. Along the way, they had to encounter days of harsh weather – long and frequent bouts snow, rain and storms meant that it took the Venetian travellers around three and a half years to complete the journey to China. According to some historians, another possible cause of the delay was illness and it is believed that Marco Polo came down with malaria and struggled with it for more than a year.

Finally, in 1275, the Polo travellers arrived at Shangdu, China which was one of the most important cities of Kublai Khan's kingdom. The Mongol Emperor was impressed by the young Marco who had passed the rigours of such a long journey with enthusiasm and courage; as a result Marco was conscripted into service of the king. He was given a passport of gold which signified his freedom to travel across the length and breadth of the country. As he continued to gain experience and expertise in the ways of Mongol politics, Marco Polo was given increasingly more important positions in the state – once he served as an ambassador representing the Kublai Khan's kingdom to another country and at another time he became the Governor of the city of Yangzhou.

The Journey to Persia

It was not long before Kublai Khan decided to entrust the Polo travellers and chiefly Marco with an important mission – they were to escort a Mongol princess to a Persian kingdom whose prince she was supposed to wed. This meant covering a great distance not only crossing naturally hazardous routes but also dangers like adverse weather and gangs of pirates. However, Marco Polo, his father and uncle were by this time keen to leave the Mongol kingdom. They were not only eager to go back to the land of their birth but they sensed that the ongoing political developments in China would soon take an unfavourable turn since the Chinese nobles were growing resentful of the Mongol Rulers. Thus, after seventeen years in the court of Kublai Khan, the Polos were ready to leave China and the plan was that after safely seeing the Mongol princess to Persia – where she was to wed the Khan's great-nephew – they would leave for their home in Venice.

A massive fleet of fourteen huge boats, six hundred crew including the personal retinue of the Princess and the Polo brothers left from a port in Southern China in 1292. The ships initially sailed southwards, passing by the coasts of Indonesia and Sri Lanka from where it turned westward, sailing past the coasts of India and then turning northwest to head for the Strait of Hormuz in the Persian Gulf which would bring them to their destination.

Despite all the preparations with which the Armada had set forth from China, the long arduous voyage had taken its toll and from the original six hundred passengers, only eighteen were able to make it to the destination. Among the survivors was the Princess who upon finding that her betrothed had already died during the long journey, decided to marry his son instead.

The Account of His Travels

The Polo brothers, in their turn, were relieved to have come closer to their homeland and soon left for Venice upon their landing at the Strait of Hormuz. Not much is known about Marco Polo's life in this period, though he is believed to have married a Venetian woman named Donata and even had three daughters by her.

However, a life of action once again enveloped Marco and soon he got involved in a war with the city state of Genoa and even signed up with the Venetian army. However, the war did not go well for Venice and at the end of it in 1298, Marco Polo found himself imprisoned by the Genoese soldiers.

It was here, in prison, that Marco Polo began to think back upon his life of travel and adventure and decided to do something to document his experiences. Fortunately, he was able to find in a fellow prisoner named Rustichello a sympathetic listener who was just as willing to act as a writer. Thus, over the course of two years of his imprisonment in the Genoese cell, Marco Polo dictated an account of his travels on the various roads of Central Asia and especially of his life in the kingdom of the Great Khan and in different parts of China. In all the trio, Marco Polo with his father and uncle had spent some twenty-fours on the road, passing through strikingly beautiful lands of the Middle East, Central Asia and China but also encountering some of the most dangerous paths in this part of the world. The result of these reminiscences was a book titled, *Travels of Marco Polo*, which was first published in French and later known as *Il Milione* in Italian, which translates as *The Thousand*.

The Travels of Marco Polo

Though the book went on to have a great impact on readers in Europe, there was a downside to the immense popularity too. Because of the huge demand, Marco's book suffered from hasty translations and editing done by the monks and printers who reproduced it indiscriminately. This eventually resulted in a whole lot of different versions of *Travels of Marco Polo*, with some historians putting the estimate at a whopping 150 different versions.

The book dictated by Marco Polo is something like a geographical description of various Asian countries. It is planned into chapters dealing with specific regions of the continent and in each of these, Marco Polo gives a detailed account of the physical, political and cultural attributes of the land. Thus, for example, in a chapter devoted to a place in Indonesia, he goes on to describe the economic practices, agriculture methods, military arrangements as well as the religious ways, the burial system and even the sexual practices of the area. All this made his accounts of places and kingdoms highly interesting – they were not just full of dry statistics but alive with local colour and vivid descriptions, which not surprisingly was responsible for the immense popularity of the book.

Legacy of Marco Polo

Though there is no doubt about the huge popularity that the *Travels of Marco Polo* enjoyed in its lifetime, critical recognition was entirely another matter. Historians have been quick to doubt the authenticity of Marco Polo's accounts of his travels through China and other Asian countries. Passages from the book sometimes seem rather fantastic like the description of men with tails and there seem to be too many encounters with cannibalistic tribes through the journeys. Again some historians point out that the exaggerated description of the different places and cultures in the book are a proof that Marco Polo himself never went as far east as China but are the result of what he picked up from other travellers and merchants to the East.

Supporters of Marco Polo on their part defend him by pointing out that since he never wrote the book himself, it is possible that the fanciful bits in the book are the result of the scribe Rustichello's overactive imagination. It is quite likely that Rustichello embellished the travel accounts with exaggerated details of his own which he thought would contribute to the popularity of the book.

Again some critics base their disbelief in Marco Polo's travels on the absence of any mention of typically Chinese practices like foot-binding of women, use of chopsticks for eating food and above all, significant landmarks like the Great Wall of China. However, loyalists point out that the really major parts of the Great Wall hadn't yet been built by the time he visited and so no mention of the Wall exists in the book.

Charges of fabrication in fact continued to dog Marco Polo till the end of his life. In 1324, when he lay on his deathbed, he was asked to confess the account of his travels as being false. But Marco Polo simply said that all that he had authored in the book was not even half of what he had really witnessed during the course of his adventures.

No matter what the discrepancies are, Marco Polo's books had a major impact on the knowledge systems of contemporary Europe. The Venetian's travels through China under the patronage and sometimes in service of the Mongol Emperor made him the first European to explore the length and breadth of this Asian land and to see its people and society in such close quarters.

Over the course of his journeys through Central Asia and across China, Marco Polo came across many products then unknown to the Western world. The most important among these was silk, porcelain, coal and the compass. It was also in China that Marco Polo first came across paper money and the concept when introduced in Europe through his book, turned out to create quite a stir at the time. No wonder then in his book, China comes across as a land of amazing scientific and technological progress, from which Europe could perhaps learn a thing or two.

Finally, the account of Marco Polo's travels had a significant impact on the way the world was imagined – the descriptions of the lands and trade routes in his book resulted in Europe's first maps of Asia. But what was still more important for the history of human exploration was that his travels inspired many other adventurers to set out for uncharted territories. Christopher Columbus, one of the greatest explorers of the world, was thought to own a copy of Marco Polo's book and made annotations in the margins. In fact, it is famously believed that the great Genoese explorer was actually searching for India based on Marco's described location, when he landed on the West Indies and hence came upon the New World in 1492.

So despite the fact that the veracity of his accounts of journeys continues to be in question, there remains no doubt about its lasting influence. For many centuries since its first publication in sometime around 1300, the *Travels of Marco Polo* continued to exist as the only kind of regional geography of Asia. Even today, his book stands among the greatest records of geographic exploration in the history of human knowledge.

□

5

Zheng He

(1371-1433)

Much of the history of human exploration has been written from the point of view of Europeans. Not surprisingly then the explorers like Christopher Columbus and Thomas Cook have been hailed as pioneers of geographic discovery. It is only now that the world is getting acquainted with the names of explorers from other cultures who have ventured through uncharted territories at different times in human history. And one of these belongs to 15th century Chinese admiral and explorer Zheng He who commanded seven voyages of the Treasure Fleets of the Imperial Army which sailed through the Indian Ocean and even the Western Pacific.

Early Life of Zheng He

Zheng He was born as Ma Ho in China's south-western Yunan province around 1371. Son to a Haji, a devout Muslim who had made a pilgrimage to the Mecca, Ma Ho was given the family name Ma in honour of the Prophet Mohammad. In around 1381 when the Chinese army invaded Yuan in an attempt to seize control over the remote outer provinces, ten year-old Ma Ho was captured along with other kids of his family and sold into slavery. When he became thirteen, Ma Ho in keeping with the practices of the times, was castrated so that he could be placed as a servant to the Imperial family. Thus began Ma Ho's service in the household of Prince Zhu Di, the fourth son of the Chinese Emperor.

Very soon however Ma Ho came into the notice of Prince Zhu. Towering at seven feet, Ma Ho proved himself as keen a student of the art of war as that of state affairs and it was only a matter of time before he found himself serving as a close official aide of the Prince. Ma Ho was given the title of Cheng Ho when the latter's horse was killed in a battle outside the palace of Zhenglunba. In the newer Chinese Pinyin dialect, Chen is translated as Zheng and that is how the warrior is widely known today.

Rise to Power

That Zheng He was highly skilled as a warrior and diplomat was well known by now and he received yet another moniker, San Bao which translates as, "Three Jewels". However, Zheng's rise to power was cemented when his patron Prince Zhu became the Imperial Emperor of China in 1402. Within a year, Zhen was elevated into the post of the Admiral of the Imperial navy and given the task of carrying out explorations throughout the Indian Ocean. This was the first time in Chinese history that a eunuch had risen to such great heights in the country's politics and military.

In his capacity of the Admiral, Zheng He was now responsible for China's maritime expeditions whose aim was to extend the influence of China to all the coasts and countries of the Indian Ocean and even Western Pacific. For this purpose, a plan to construct Treasure Fleets was finalized which would embark on seven voyages under the command of Zheng He.

1405-07, The First Voyage

The first of the Treasure Fleets was a grand affair, involving painstaking planning and large-scale construction. In all, the first Treasure Fleet consisted of 62 ships which in turn included different kinds of vessels to carry out different functions. Four of the largest of these 62 ships were flagship vessels; assembled at Nanjing along the Yangtze River, they were built according to massive dimensions, unheard of till then – measuring an incredible 400 feet in length and 120 feet in width – something that even the Europeans had not yet figured out to do in this age.

The rest of the fleet included ships to carry provisions and fresh water for the crew and which were known as water ships. Then again there were huge 139 feet-long vessels where the only cargo consisted of horses and were known as horse ships. Other vessels were constructed and fitted for different functions like carrying troop transport as well war-ships for both offensive and defensive military actions. No less important part of the cargo was thousands of tonnes of Chinese products which would form the basis of establishing commercial relations with the traders in India. Finally, the fleet set sail in the autumn of 1405 with a carrying around 27,800 men in various capacities.

The first of the 15th century Chinese Treasure Fleets is not only remarkable for their planning and dimensions but also because they showcased the most advanced of Chinese inventions of the times. The ships of the fleet were fitted with the compass which had already been invented in China in the 11th century and now constituted an important navigational instrument. Also Chinese mathematicians had already found a means to calculate latitude of a location with reference to the North Star in the Northern Hemisphere and the Southern Cross in the Southern Hemisphere. Both visual and audio means were used to facilitate communication between the ships of the fleet – like lanterns, flags and banners as well as gongs and bells, not to mention live couriers like carrier pigeons. Finally, there were sophisticated means of measuring time – through the use of graduated incense sticks – so that an entire day could be divided into ten watches of 2.4 hours each. In this way, Zheng He ensured that the most modern of Chinese scientific and technological knowledge of the times would be used for his fleet and in the process boosted the chances of the expedition's success.

The first Treasure Fleet set sail with the ultimate intention of reaching Calicut, an important port on the south-western coast of the Indian subcontinent which was well known at the time as a major trading centre and an important source of coveted products especially spices. India was already known to the Chinese nobility and intelligentsia as the land of many riches, mainly through the writings of 7th century Chinese Buddhist pilgrim and scholar Huen Tsang or more accurately Xuangzang, whose desire to travel to the land of Buddha had brought him through Central Asia into India. Under Zheng He's command, the first Treasure Fleet sailed through the Indian Ocean, stopping at the ports of Java, Malacca and Vietnam till it turned west and came upon the famous trading ports of southwest India, Calicut and Cochin. This was late 1406 and the Chinese voyagers stayed in the ports till early 1407 when they took advantage of the change in direction of the monsoon winds to sail back home to China. Over the course of less than a year, the Chinese expedition sold their own wares for Indian as well international commodities for which the trading ports of India were famous. On their way back, the Treasure Fleet ran into some pirates off the coast of Sumatra and were forced to engage in a long-drawn out battle. Finally, the pirates were defeated, their chieftain captured and with these victories under his belt, in 1407 Zheng He re-entered his native capital of Nanjing to a triumphant welcome.

1407-09, The Second Voyage

The Chinese Emperor was keen to build on the success of the commercial gains of the First Voyage to India and with this in mind, he ordered that the Treasure Fleet soon get ready for a second voyage which started in 1407 and returned two years later 1409. Though Zheng He was not part of this voyage – having been given the responsibility of supervising the repairs of a temple dedicated to a venerated Goddess in China – his lessons from the First Voyage proved invaluable to the second expedition and they returned with substantial commercial success.

1409-11, The Third Voyage

Zheng He was soon ordered to command a third voyage of the Treasure Fleets but this time the purpose was more material rather than merely adventurous. Even then the expedition consisted of still more men, around 30,000, though slightly fewer number of ships at 48. The orders from the Chinese Emperor were to establish rudimentary trading posts, replete with storehouses and camps to store goods along the route to India so that Chinese trading interests could not only be established but well protected from local competitors and authorities. Not all kingdoms took kindly to this attempt at settlements by the Chinese and it was only a matter of time before Zheng He's men came into confrontation with local kings. One such instance took place in Ceylon where the king tried to use force against the Chinese contingent but was defeated and taken as a prisoner to Nanjing.

1413-15, The Fourth Voyage

This skirmish with the kingdom of Ceylon did nothing to dampen the trading determination of the Chinese Emperor and in late 1412, Zhu ordered Zheng He to prepare for a fourth voyage of the Treasure Fleets. This time the expedition was to include 28,560 men and the maximum number of ships yet, at 63. This time though the destination was not Calicut on the Indian south-western coast but a trading port still further north – Hormuz on the Persian Gulf which was famous as the city of fabulous wealth and luxurious good, especially pearls and other jewels which the Chinese Emperor was keen to add to his personal riches. Considering the brave, experienced and intelligent commander that he was, Zheng He succeeded in the Imperial mission this time too and not only brought back exotic goods and precious stones to gladden the Chinese Emperor's heart but also pushed the limits of the world as known to the Chinese at that time. In fact, from the Persian port, the expedition split into smaller contingents and while some carried out trading activities, others under the guidance of the adventurous Zheng, sailed south exploring the eastern coast of Africa as far as Mozambique.

Zheng He's success as a commander of the Treasure Fleets were not just limited to geographical or commercial. He also did a great deal to improve the international relations of the Imperial Chinese Court. With his background as a diplomat, Zheng He ensured that the Chinese remained on cordial terms with all the kingdoms that the expedition passed on the way. To this end, on the Fourth Voyage, he not only encouraged the local kingdoms to send their emissaries to China but himself brought back diplomats from several countries when returning from the voyages to the Chinese capital of Nanjing.

1417-19, The Fifth Voyage

In 1417, the Treasure Fleets set sail again for the Persian Gulf to complete China's diplomatic initiative – all the emissaries and ambassadors from other countries who had accompanied Zheng He to the Imperial Court in the Fourth Voyage were now to be returned to their native kingdoms on the way. The diplomatic gains of this mission were significant – China had not only made its presence felt on the southern and western parts of the Indian subcontinent and extended it till Africa but had convinced most of the countries on the way it was in their benefit to maintain cordial commercial and military relations with China.

1421-22, The Sixth Voyage

The commercial and diplomatic successes of the Fourth and Fifth Voyages had turned Africa into prime trading destination for the Chinese Emperor. He was not only hooked to the riches and precious stones offered by the traders of Hormuz but eager to bring home the wealth and exotic products to be found in other trading ports of Africa. Zheng He completed most of his Emperor's requisitions and returned home in late 1421 but it was not before next year that the remaining part of the expedition would arrive in China.

1431-33, The Seventh Voyage

The decade long gap between the Sixth and Seventh Voyages of the Treasure Fleets owes to significant changes in the Imperial Court of China. Shortly after Zheng He's arrival from the Sixth Voyage, in 1424 his mentor Emperor Zhu Di died and the crown passed on to the latter's son, Zhu Gaozhi. The new Emperor was not a keen patron of maritime exploration and trading and thus Zhu Gaozhi ordered that there were to be no more voyages by the

Treasure Fleets – the ship builders and sailors were disbanded and the Admiral of the Imperial Chinese Navy was compelled to take up a new appointment as the military commander of Nanjing.

However, Zhu Gaozhi was not destined to rule for very long – in 1426 at the age of just 26, he died and the rule passed on to his son, Zhu Zhanji. With a keen sense of exploration, the new Emperor was more like his grandfather than his father and it was not long before the Treasure Fleet was brought back in service and in 1430 the brave and experienced Admiral Zheng He was asked to prepare to command it again. The purpose of the Seventh Voyage of the Fleet was going to be more of a diplomatic than a commercial one – Zheng He was given the express order of reviving amicable relations with the kingdoms of Siam and Malacca which were important trading partners of the Chinese on the Indian Ocean. Because of the long gap in expeditions, it took more than a year for the Treasure Fleet to be outfitted properly and finally in 1431 it was ready to embark on its Seventh Voyage with around 27,500 men and the largest ever contingent of vessels, an astounding hundred ships.

The Seventh Voyage was not only going to be the Treasure Fleet's last but that of Zheng He's too. According to some accounts, the Admiral died on the return journey of the Fleet while other historical anecdotes mention that he passed away after his arrival in China.

Zheng He's Legacy

No matter what the exact date, with Zheng He's death, the era of maritime exploration drew to a close in China. For one the later emperors were disinterested in furthering commercial or diplomatic relations with other countries; equally importantly the country no longer had a maritime expert and statesman of Zheng He's calibre to benefit from. Thus, not only the Treasure Fleet came to be disbanded but for long the construction of ocean-going vessels was put on hold in China.

And yet Zheng He's explorations had reaped rich rewards for the country. He had found the route to most lucrative trading ports through the Indian Ocean, the foremost of them being Calicut in India and Hormuz in the Persian Gulf. This was almost a century before Vasco da Gama became the first European to reach the Indian port by sea. In fact, based on the oral traditions of the Aborigine people in Australia and the archaeological excavation of Chinese artefacts there, it is even possible that one of the contingents of the Treasure Fleet may have touched the Australian shores.

Finally, Zheng He's achievements were not only commercial in nature – his diplomatic initiatives secured the goodwill of several kings along lucrative trading routes on the Indian Ocean and ensured commercial success of Chinese traders. No less important was the fact that Zheng He utilized the most modern of Chinese technological innovations for his nautical ventures with the result that scientific innovations and knowledge received a fillip during his time.

It would be another hundred odd years since Zheng He's death that China would come into notice of the European explorers and traders. In 1488, the Spaniard Bartholomew Dias would make the momentous sea journey around the Cape of Good Hope, thus opening up a faster, nautical alternative to the long, hazardous land journey that Europeans had till now depended on to visit the best trading centres of Indian coasts. Soon enough in 1498 Vasco da Gama would land on the port of Calicut and in the process jump-start the rush of European nations all looking for a piece of the vast Asian market. But till then Chinese influence on the trading centres of the Indian Ocean would reign supreme, thanks to the adventurous and entrepreneurial spirit of Admiral Zheng He.

□

6

John Cabot

(C. 1450-1499)

15th century, Europe was a time of great exploration and new knowledge. Known as the Age of Discovery, this period was as much marked by a flowering of humanistic sciences and arts as by a competition for claiming the newly-discovered lands on the globe. Navigators, seafarers and travellers from the countries of Spain, Italy, Portugal, France and England were in a rush to explore the unchartered corners of land and sea. This is because discovery of new lands and a European country's ownership of them meant that the new ruler could utilize the natural resources of the land which could range from immensely useful products like coal and spice to lucrative trade items like silk and precious stones. It was in this political and economic context that an Italian-born explorer named John Cabot set off to find a direct and quicker route to Asia and he stumbled upon the shores of Canada, thus effectively becoming the first early modern European to discover North America.

Early Life

John Cabot is actually the English name of Giovanni Caboto who was born in city of Gaeta or Castiglione Chiavarese in Italy, sometime before 1450. Some years later however his family moved to Venice and young Giovanni grew up imbibing the rich and varied commercial culture of this Italian city. It was not long before

Giovanni showed promise as a trader and eventually he found success as one of the most respected members of the mercantile community of Venice. Historians know this because the name of John Cabot appears in the Venetian records in 1471 which marks the year of his entry into the religious confraternity of St. John the Evangelist. Since this was one of the city's most elite confraternities, it is likely that John Cabot was already an established name in the community.

According to some historical sources, Giovanni Caboto was part of the lucrative spice trade which at that time traversed from Venice to the Mediterranean. Because of his involvement in the spice trade, he was a regular visitor to the Levant or eastern Mediterranean many times and indeed may have travelled as far as Mecca, which was the nerve centre for trade in Oriental and Western goods at that time. Though some historians doubt whether he had actually visited Mecca, it is usually agreed that John Cabot had better knowledge of the origins of the exotic eastern commodities like spices and silks than most European traders at that time in Venice.

To bring in better returns from his spice trade, Giovanni began thinking of looking for alternative routes to travel to Asia by taking the westward route instead of depending on the long hazardous eastwards land route through the Mediterranean, Persia and Central Asia. A new westward sea route would not only cut down the travel time but even do away with intermediaries in the Levant who charged high percentages of the trading value. This was a common aspiration among the best explores of the time, including Christopher Columbus who too landed on the Caribbean shores, thinking that he had discovered the westward route to the Indies. In order to equip himself for his explorations, Giovanni thus began learning map making as well as navigation at sea.

Preparations for the Voyage

However, it would be still sometime before Giovanni managed to turn his plans of seeking direct sea route to Asia a reality. The decades before Caboto's first voyage are rather vague. According to some sources, he found his way to Valencia and then to Seville in Spain. In fact, he may have been in the same place as Christopher Columbus in 1493, as the latter passed through Valencia on his way to meet the King of Spain, after his western voyage of 1492 and his mistaken arrival upon the 'Indies'.

It was also probably around this time that Giovanni also got married to a woman named Mattea and had three sons by her, who were named Ludovico, Sebastion and Sancto. Around this time, he was contracted to build a bridge over the Guadalquivir River in Seville. He even worked on it for five months but the funding by the city government ran out and consequently the project was shelved. However, Giovanni probably continued to make a decent living as a map-maker. This is because since skilled cartographers were in great demand in those times when the very success of nautical expeditions could depend upon the accuracy of maps, sea and land routes. Also the competition among the great sailing nations like Spain, Portugal, England and Italy was so great that an expedition which was successful in finding new lands or sea routes stood to benefit from huge amounts of monetary reward as well as national recognition.

The First Voyage

In late 1495, Giovanni arrived at Bristol whereupon he probably began to be known by his English name John Cabot. Bristol was one of the most important ports of England and was much favoured by maritime explorers as the starting point for voyages across the North Atlantic. When at Bristol, Cabot set out to meet English officials and through them persuaded the Crown that England needed to get its act together before Spanish explorers landed on different parts of the New World and established colonies under the flag of Spain. Cabot's solution was to adopt a more northerly approach than the one taken by Christopher Columbus and in this way seek a faster alternative route to Asia.

On the 5 March 1496, Cabot received letters patent from King Henry-VII according to which the Crown authorized Cabot and his son to set out on a voyage under the English flag and to carry out trade of whatever goods he could bring back in the English market. All that is known about Cabot's first voyage comes from a letter written by a Bristol merchant named John Day to Christopher Columbus. Dated in the winter of 1497-98, the letter largely talks about Cabot's 1497 voyage but in an aside, Day notes that in the first voyage Cabot and his crew was held up by bad weather for many days and since their provisions were running dangerously low, Cabot decided to turn back.

The Second Voyage

Soon however Cabot was able to commandeer a second crew of fifteen men together with a small ship named Mathew which some historical sources was a corruption of the Italian name of his wife Mattea. In May 1497, Cabot and his ship set sail from the port of Bristol.

In June 1497, Cabot and his crew made landfall – he had arrived upon the eastern coast of Canada though at that time, he believed that he had finally found a way across the ocean to the north-eastern part of Asian. The modern-day equivalent of Cabot's landfall is most likely the area that comprises Southern Labrador, the Cape Breton Island and Island of Newfoundland in Canada. In fact, it was Cabot's later report to the King of England, Henry-VII that he had come upon, "newfound land", that led to the Canadian province being named so.

Cabot was eager to make good his discovery in commercial sense too – thus he went ashore and even came upon signs of human habitation like the remains of a fire, a human trail, nets and a wooden tool but could find no people to trade in goods. In any case, he claimed the land in the name of King of England, though he is believed to have planted both the English and Venetian flags on the earth of the newly-discovered land.

Before returning, Cabot carried out explorations of the area and even gave names to various landmarks of the region; some of these were Island of St. John, Cape Discovery, St. George's Cape, England's Cape as well as the Trinity Islands. After this he set sail for Bristol and docked in the English port in August 1497.

Upon his return to England, Cabot went straight to King Henry-VII and gave him the good news of the discovery of, "new-found lands", during the voyage. Not surprisingly, Cabot was hailed as a hero and received a good deal of financial reward as well as praise for the results of his voyage.

Cabot's Third Voyage

Flush with the success of his Second Voyage, Cabot began making plans of another expedition and towards the end of 1497, he went to Henry-VII to discuss the matter. The Italian explorer proposed to the king that he be allowed to have a ship and the permission to make another voyage across the North Atlantic Ocean so as to make larger territorial gains in the name of the Crown. One highlight of the purported journey was to travel further westwards than the place of his first landfall until he reached the island of Japan or Cipangu as it was known then.

In February 1498, the King of England issued letters patent for the third voyage, and Cabot was able to get together five ships and 200 men as crew. At least one of the ships was believed to be carrying merchandise, including cloth, caps, lace points and other "trifles". This suggests that the expedition hoped to engage in trade and once the ships were fitted with men and provisions, Cabot set off from Bristol in May of the same year.

John Cabot's third voyage however was not to be as successful as his second. Within a couple of months, one of the five ships of Cabot's fleet was severely damaged due to bad weather and had to be docked at a port in Ireland. Though the actual details of the rest of the expedition have been lost to obscurity, even the remaining ships did not seem to fare better. No records exist of the expedition making it back to England and by 1499 it was assumed that Cabot himself had been lost to the sea.

Sebastian Cabot, one of John Cabot's sons, is believed to have later made at least one voyage to North America in 1508, looking for the Northwest Passage, a sea route connecting the Atlantic and Pacific Oceans which passes through the Arctic Ocean, along the northern coast of North America and through the Canadian Arctic

Archipelago. Another probable aim was the re-tracing of Magellan's voyage around the world but eventually Sebastian Cabot's voyage came to be involved in search for silver along the Río de la Plata which is the estuary formed by the confluence of the Uruguay River and the Paraná River on the south-eastern coast of South America.

Cabot's Legacy

John Cabot or Giovanni Caboto is now considered the first modern European to have arrived on the shores of North America. Though the Viking explorer Leif Eriksson had found a passage westward from Greenland and landed on the eastern coast of Canada much earlier than Cabot, no one had sought to build upon the Scandinavian explorer's success.

Again though only a few years before Christopher Columbus in 1492, had landed on the shores of Caribbean islands, he did not venture northward into the mainland and was thus unaware that the land constituted an entirely different continent which today is known as North American. John Cabot on the other hand had not only landed on the eastern coast of Canadian mainland but paved the way for the colonization of the, "newfound lands", and other colonies in North America, first by England and later by France.

Additionally, his swifter journey as compared to that of other explorers to the New World proved the existence of a shorter route across the North Atlantic Ocean. He reasoned that if he started travelling from a northerly latitude, where the longitudes were much closer together, he would take comparatively lesser time to go across the Atlantic Ocean.

The Cabot Project

The significance of Cabot's journeys for the history of modern European discovery of North America can be gauged from the ongoing Cabot Project. This is an international and collaborative project that was launched in July 2009 to investigate the Bristol discovery voyages of the late-15th and early-16th centuries and especially those undertaken by the Venetian adventurer, John Cabot.

The source of the Cabot Project can be traced to claims by Dr. Ruddock, formerly a Reader at Birkbeck College, University of London, that she had evidence of voyage dates that would revolutionise contemporary understanding of Europe's encounter with North America in the decades immediately following 1492. However, Ruddock never published her findings and before her death in 2005, ordered that her all notes be destroyed.

In 2006, Dr. Evans Jones of the University of Bristol and his associates decided to look for Dr. Ruddock's sources and notes and this came to take shape as the Cabot Project. Some of the most significant findings of the Cabot Project include knowledge of a Bristol merchant named William Weston who was the first Englishman to lead an expedition to North America in 1499, information that Cabot returned from his third voyage to England in the spring of 1500 instead of dying at sea, evidence that part of Cabot's journeys were funded by an Italian bank in London and that Carbonear, one of the earliest settlements to be established in Canada may have been the location of the Church and religious community that was established in 1498 by Cabot's supporter and companion, Fra Giovanni Antonio de Carbonariis.

The Cabot Trail

Though John Cabot is not known today as one of iconic explorers of human history – in the manner of Christopher Columbus or Edmund Hillary – nevertheless his legacy exists in a far more immediate way. The 60-mile-wide channel running between south-western Newfoundland and northern Cape Breton Island is now known as Cabot Strait. These include various features like the Cape Discovery, Island of St. John, St. George's Cape, Trinity Islands and England's Cape. Throughout the history of Canada and Newfoundland, the Cabot Strait has been a strategically important waterway. Even today it is a significant international shipping route and constitutes the main water route that connects the inland ports on the Great Lakes and St. Lawrence Seaway with the Atlantic Ocean.

The Cabot Strait in fact provides the basis for an extremely beautiful and much-prized trail in Canada also known as the Cabot Trail. Named one of the best road trips in the world by Lonely Planet, the trail winds through fascinating landscapes, along the Margaree River, and through stunning rugged highlands of the Cape Breton Highlands National Park of Canada. The northern portion of the Cabot Trail runs through Cape Breton Highlands National Park. Both the eastern and western sections of the Trail pass along the rugged coastline and thus offers amazing vistas of the Atlantic Ocean. The south-western section of the Trail runs through the Margaree River Valley and then moves along the Bras d'Or Lake. No wonder then that the Cabot Trail is considered one of the world's most scenic destination areas.

Completed in 1932, the Cabot Trail strung erstwhile isolated fishing hamlets into a loop that runs for around 300 km. In fact, the Cabot Trail is the sole trunk secondary highway in the Canadian province of Nova Scotia that does not have a signed route designation. All along the trail, there are only road signs displaying a mountain logo unique to this route. Today, the Cabot Trail connects eight different communities, ranging from the Acadian Region, to Irish and Scottish settlements. Each has its own interesting history and culture and is a major draw to the travellers who explore the Cabot Trail. Equally attractive are the many outdoors and adventure activities that the mountains, valleys, lakes, rivers and forests of the Cabot Trail offers to its visitors.

□

7

Christopher Columbus

(1451-1506)

If there is one name that evokes the spirit and excitement of geographical exploration from the Age of Discovery, that name is of Christopher Columbus. In 1492, his ship arrived on the coast of modern-day West Indies and – though his main purpose of the voyage was to find a westward sea route from Europe to India – he actually became the first modern European to come upon the continent of America which was eventually hailed as the, 'New World', and turned into a much sought-after destination for European explorers, merchants and rulers.

The Age of Discovery

Europe in the 15th century was an exciting time to live in. Under the wave of Renaissance, old theological systems of knowledge were being brushed aside to make space for a new secular, humanist and progressive way of thinking. One of the most important pursuits to benefit was that of geographical exploration – with the advances of science and mathematics, navigators and adventurers felt ready to stride through unchartered territories on land and sea.

At the same, time there was a definite commercial angle to all this hunger for exploration. Leaders of several European kingdoms funded expeditions abroad in the hope that explorers would find vast undiscovered lands and take control over their resources. Portugal and Spain especially were at the forefront of the race to find new wealthy lands as well as alternate routes for the ones that were already known about. China, India and the Malacca Islands for instance were famous as sources of like silk, spices, gemstones and other precious commodities while Africa was becoming a source of slaves. Portugal had small fast ships known as caravels which sailed along the African coast, carrying spices, gold, slaves and other goods from Asia and Africa to Europe. And though Spain was initially caught up with its war against the Moors, once it managed to expel Muslims and Jews from its territory, it turned its attention to international trade and colonization by sea.

Early Life of Christopher Columbus

Born in 1451, Christopher Columbus was the son of a wool weaver Domenico Colombo and his wife Susanna Fontanarossa who lived in Genoa, a part of present-day Italy. Though growing up in a middle-class household, young Christopher seemed to have got a good education since he was able to speak several languages as an adult. Moreover, he had considerable knowledge of classical literature and was acquainted with the works of ancient geographers like Ptolemy and Marinus.

However, Christopher was not to be satisfied with a life of mere learning and when just fourteen, he found berth on a merchant ship. Through the 1470s, he went on numerous trading voyages to ports along the Aegean Sea, Northern Europe, and perhaps even to Iceland. Columbus continued his journeys until on one occasion his ship was attacked by French privateers; though the boat sank, young Columbus was able to float on a scrap of wood and make his way to the shore.

After his miraculous escape, Columbus headed for Lisbon where his brother Bartolomeo was a map-maker. There Christopher settled down for a while and began studying the various sciences associated with maritime exploration like navigation, mathematics, astronomy and cartography. Not surprisingly then, it was here that

Columbus first felt the outlines of a remarkable idea taking shape in his brain – that since the earth was round, a westward sea route would take a ship from Europe to the wealthy lands of the Indies.

Around this time also Columbus also got married to a woman named Filipa Moniz Perestrello and in 1480, his son Diego was born. However in 1485, his wife died and after that Columbus became keen to head out on the sea again. From Lisbon thus, Columbus and his son moved to Spain which was then on the cutting edge of navigational science and enterprise.

Plans for the Voyage

Though Oriental commodities like spices and silk were much prized by the European traders, getting them from the source countries was another matter altogether. The overland route to China and India through Africa, Middle East and Central Asia was extremely long and hazardous. Apart from harsh terrain and severe weather conditions, there was the danger of robbers and diseases. The Portuguese tried to solve the problem by charting a sea route southwards along the West African coast and then going around the Cape of Good Hope, till they reached the south-western coast of India.

But since the Portuguese aggressively guarded this sea route, Spain and other countries were on the lookout for alternate routes to reach the Asia, especially the spice-rich Islands. And it was to meet this demand that Columbus began thinking of a westward voyage from Europe. He made several representations to the Spanish rulers but it was not before 1491 – once Spain had defeated the Moors – that Columbus's plans received some consideration.

At the time, Spain was ruled by Ferdinand of Aragon and Isabella of Castile – both were devout Catholics and thought that Columbus's discovery of new lands would be a good way to spread Catholic Christianity. While Columbus also thought alike, far more pressing was his desire for fame, riches and recognition as the pioneer of a new sea route to the Indies. And Columbus knew that for his plans to succeed, it was necessary for the Spanish royals to see the commercial advantage of his proposed journey. He tried to convince the royal patrons that an alternate westwards sea route would give Spain control of a new path, beat Portuguese competition for trade and even bring riches from all the lands he found on the way. In return, he asked to be allowed to take ten per cent of whatever riches he found, be granted a noble title and the governorship of any new land that the expedition may encounter.

First Voyage

With the funds from Spanish rulers, Columbus set out to prepare his ships and crew. He managed to gather a crew of 104 men and three ships to form his fleet. Finally, on August 3, 1492, the Nina, Pinta and Santa Maria left the harbour of Lisbon to sail for the western seas. Though the expedition was forced to make a brief stop at the Canary Islands to carry out some minor repairs and restock supplies, soon enough the ships were on their way to cross the Atlantic Ocean.

However, not all was smooth sailing for Columbus. Many of his crew came down with illnesses during the voyage and even died from lack of food and water. After many weeks of arduous journey, in the dawn of October 12, 1492, Rodrigo de Triana sighted land and Columbus ordered the ships to be anchored at what is now the Bahamas. In this way, Columbus was the first European to come upon the islands comprising the Americas, though it was not so known at the time; moreover he believed that he had found Asia and thus he named the new land San Salvador. When the search of the place did not yield any riches that he had pledged to get his royal patrons, Columbus decided to continue to explore the neighbouring islands and in this way he discovered the places which comprise modern-day Cuba and Haiti, which together was then named Hispaniola.

Despite having found land, Columbus's troubles were far from over. On November 21, 1492, one of the ships, Pinta, and its crew seceded from the fleet to carry out their own exploration. Unfortunately, another ship, the Santa Maria, got caught up in a storm and was badly damaged. Since the remaining ship, the Nina, could not accommodate all the men from Santa Maria, Columbus decided to leave around forty of his crew members at Hispaniola at a hastily-built fort named Navidad and then set sail for Spain. On March 15, 1493, Columbus returned to his adopted country having completed the first voyage to the west.

The Second Voyage

Fresh from the success of his first voyage in finding new land, Columbus had little problem in getting approval for another sea journey on the same westward route. This time he planned to claim the newly-discovered lands in the name of Spain and establish some sort of colony there. Above all, he wanted to keep looking for the fabled wealth of the Orient since he firmly believed that he had come upon the 'Indies', on his last westward journey.

On November 3, some members of Columbus's crew members sighted land and they came upon three more islands which correspond to present-day Dominica, Guadeloupe, and Jamaica. Columbus at the time thought that he had come upon the islands off Japan and continued to look for riches. When he found none, he decided to make for Hispaniola and check on the men he had left there after the first voyage. Upon reaching the island of Hispaniola, Columbus found that the men had been killed by the indigenous population in retaliation of ill-treatment of the local tribes. Columbus decided to take matters in his own hand and after an intense campaign, he seized control of the whole of Hispaniola and then left his brothers Bartolomeo and Diego behind to rebuild the colony which was now to be named Santo Domingo. With this victory, he set sail for Spain in March 1496, and landed in Cadiz on July 31, thus wrapping up his second voyage.

Since Columbus had not been able to find the promised riches for his royal patrons, he ordered that around 500 natives enslaved from the newly-discovered lands be sent to Queen Isabella. However, the queen was appalled at such a 'gift'. This is because she believed that the people from the newly claimed Spanish lands were technically subjects of Spain who could not be subject to such inhuman treatment. And thus the queen rejected Columbus's offer of slaves and ordered that they be returned.

The Third Voyage

Despite Columbus's growing fame as an explorer, he still felt frustrated about not being able to find the riches such as silk, spices, gold and pearls that the Asian countries were known for. And goaded by this thought, Columbus embarked on yet another voyage began on May 30, 1498. This time he planned to take a more southern route than he had done previously, thinking that going further south would bring him upon the Indies. Instead, he found the lands which are today known as Trinidad and Tobago, Grenada, and Margarita. More importantly during the search for China and India, he reached the mainland of South America.

After this, he planned to turn back to the colony of Hispaniola but this was not to be one of his successes. He found the fort and settlements in ruins – it turned out that Columbus's brothers had treated the indigenous population as well as the colonists with such brutality that the locals had rebelled in protest and destroyed everything. Such was the scale of the disaster that news reached Spain and a new Governor was sent to replace Columbus. The famous explorer was now arrested and sent back to Spain in disgrace. However, in the Spanish court, Columbus was able to defend himself successfully but had to give up his noble titles.

The Fourth Voyage

Though Columbus had fallen out of favour with the Spanish king, he made one last appeal for permission to go on another voyage to the New World. His petition was granted and on May 9, 1502, Columbus set off with four ships and in June that year, landed on the shores of Hispaniola. However, he was stopped from entering the Spanish colony there and thus on July 4, he continued with his journey sea. During his explorations, Columbus encountered even more places that the Europeans knew nothing about – the modern-day equivalent of these lands would be Central America and in fact in January 1503 he reached what is now known as Panama. Though finally, Columbus had found a place which had some gold, he was soon evicted by the indigenous people and even lost two of his four ships. Around this time, Columbus's expedition was beset with other problems too and after almost a year of waiting at Jamaica, he was able to commandeer a ship back to Spain on November 7, 1504.

When he reached Spain, Columbus found that his erstwhile patroness Queen Isabella had died on November 26, 1504. He once again tried to appeal to the king to return his governorship of Hispaniola but apart from allowing Columbus to petition, the Crown was in no mood to relent to any of his requests. At last Columbus settled down with his son in Seville and in May 20, 1506 died of ill health.

His Legacy

For long, Christopher Columbus was hailed as the one to "discover", the New World and the first to step on the American continent. However, modern historians, influenced by post-colonial theories, have started questioning his legacy. For one, Columbus was hardly the first human to set foot on the American soil. For centuries, the continents of both North and South American had been populated by indigenous people. And Columbus was not even the first European to land in North America – around five centuries before him, the Viking explorers had already found their way to this land through the Arctic Ocean and Leif Eriksson had become the first man from Europe to land on the east coast of Canada.

Far more serious accusations against Columbus have to do with the consequences of his, "discovery", of the New World. His arrival on the shores of Bahamas set in motion the forces of slavery and colonization. Large swathes of indigenous population in the Central and South Americas succumbed to illnesses and environmental hazards brought by the European sailors and entire tribes were decimated. Then there was the commercial and human exploitation of these lands – their native wealth was plundered, people were enslaved and finally the land was colonized.

And yet despite all the unhappy consequences, there is no denying the fact that the findings of his first voyage proved to be extremely significant for human exploration and geography. And though he was not really the first European to land in America, he was still the first to visit, stay and leave behind settlements in these new lands, with the result that the world became aware of the existence of these places. No wonder then that despite many qualifications, Columbus remains an iconic figure in the history of exploration. In the US, the national capital Washington is part of the District of Columbia and every October on the second Monday, Columbus Day is celebrated with great fanfare.

□

8

Ferdinand Magellan

(C. 1480-1521)

That the earth was round in shape and not a flat surface extending into eternity was known as far back to humans as the ancient Greeks. However, the full extent of the possibilities resulting from earth's spherical shape became clear in the Age of Discovery, when ambitious and intelligent explorers from countries like Spain, Portugal, Italy and England tried to find a westward route from Europe in an attempt to reach Asia. In this context, Ferdinand Magellan's name finds a prime spot, since he not only became the first to prove that the earth could be circled by sea but his expeditions also showed that there was much more to be discovered about the world than what was presently known.

Early Life

Born in 1480 at Sabrosa, Portugal, Ferdinand Magellan belonged to a family of known to the royalty in a minor capacity. This is why after the early death of his parents in 1490, twelve-year-old Ferdinand and his brother Diogo went to live in Lisbon at the royal court of Portugal where they were to serve as pageboys to Queen Leonara.

Living at the court, young Ferdinand got the best of educational opportunities and he started learning a great deal about geography, maritime navigation, map-making and other sciences. This desire for knowledge was partly fuelled by the contemporary flowering of nautical exploration especially in the context of fierce competition with Spain. Explorers who returned with proofs of newly-discovered lands and sea passages were not only handsomely rewarded and praised by the royalty but could also look forward to a life of popular adulation and commercial gain. No wonder then that the Portuguese court was usually abuzz with news of explorers leaving for expeditions – possibly even about the ones led by Christopher Columbus – and all this had a major impact on Magellan who increasingly became impatient to try his luck at the sea.

Rivalry for Spice Trade

Though the wave of explorations during the Age of Discovery did a lot to extend the limits of human knowledge about the planet, to a large extent, they were propelled by far more prosaic concerns – to gain a commercial advantage in the Spice Trade. In 15th century, spices from various Asian islands constituted one of the most highly-prized trading commodities in Europe. This was because spices were not only used for flavouring food but also for preserving them. Chiefly used to cover the taste of rotting meat, spices like clove, cinnamon, nutmeg and especially black pepper were regarded as highly precious items. Since spices could not be grown in the cold climate of Europe, the only way to get them was from the Asian countries where they grew, which mainly included the Spice Islands or Malaccas in modern Indonesia but also other places like southern India and Sri Lanka. And to control this trade, European kingdoms were ready to go to great lengths and spend huge amounts of money. At the time the usual route for Spice Trade for Europeans was to travel eastwards by sea or land till they arrived in Asia and at the Spice Islands. With competition heating up over the Spice Trade, one of the driving concerns for the countries involved became to look for an alternative route which would shorten the travel time. And since by now explorers were convinced of the earth's spherical shape, they reasoned that by travelling west from Europe they were bound to come upon the Spice Islands.

Another international development also provided a boost to the search for an alternative trade route for the Spice Islands. In order to bring some order into the conflict between Spain and Portugal – whose commercial rivalry over the colonial trade was threatening to become uglier – Treaty of Tordesillas was signed by both countries in 1494. According to this treaty, the world would be divided the world in half through the Atlantic Ocean – Spain would be allowed to trade with countries west of the line, including the Americas and the Portuguese could take the lands east of the line including India and the eastern half of Africa. But like all major trading countries of Europe at that time, Spain too wanted a larger piece of the Spice Trade and hence began encouraging its explorers to look for alternate routes to the Spice Islands.

Magellan's First Voyage

Though Magellan was brimming with ideas for westward travel in search of the Spice Islands, it would be some time before he could put his plans in action. However, his wish for some seafaring action was soon to come true since in 1505 he was sent by Portugal to India in support of Francisco del Almeida who was having trouble in establishing his authority as the Portuguese Viceroy. This was Magellan's first sea voyage and soon after arriving in India he was thrust into action. In 1509, Magellan found himself taking part in a battle against a local king who had rejected the practice of paying tribute to the new Portuguese Viceroy.

Over the next few years, Magellan participated in several expeditions in India and Africa where the Portuguese colonial authority had to be enforced. In 1513, Magellan set out for Morocco and joined a massive expedition of 500 ships and 1500 soldiers with the purpose of subjugating the local king for not paying the yearly tribute to the Portuguese Governor there. Though the Portuguese forces easily defeated the Moroccan soldiers, Magellan was wounded in a battle and left with a permanent limp. Even after the objective of establishing Portuguese authority had been fulfilled, Magellan stayed on in Morocco for around seven years.

Despite fighting on behalf of Portugal, eventually, Magellan fell out of favour with his rulers. In India, he had gone against Almeida's wishes when he decided to leave without the permission of the Portuguese Viceroy. Again in Morocco he was suspected to trade illegally with the Moors. When some of these charges proved to be true, Magellan was dismissed from royal service in 1514.

Move to Spain

Despite falling from royal favour, Magellan had enough faith in his exploration plans to seek a petition from the Portuguese ruler, King Manuel. In the petition, he outlined his plans for a westward voyage from Europe which because of the spherical shape of earth would eventually bring him to the Spice Islands. However, by this time, Magellan was no longer in favour with the court and his petitions were repeatedly rejected by the Portuguese king.

Frustrated Magellan renounced his citizenship of Portugal and headed for its arch-rival Spain where he hoped to have better luck in persuading the king of the worth of his plans. However, things were not so easy initially since when Magellan landed in Spain, he did not know anyone and had sparse knowledge of the language. However, as luck would have it, Magellan ran into another Portuguese expatriate named Diogo Barbosa and was soon taken under his wing. Magellan eventually married Barbosa's daughter Beatriz and after a year had a son named Rodrigo.

In the meantime, Magellan's professional life too was looking up. Through his marriage to the well-connected Barbosa family, Magellan was able to meet officials in-charge of Spain's nautical exploration and it was not long before he was able to secure a meeting with the King of Spain. King Charles I was the grandson of King Ferdinand and Queen Isabella who were famous as Columbus' patrons of his 1492 path-breaking expedition to the New World. Much like his grandparents, Charles I of Spain was also an avid supporter of new exploration ideas and thus was proved to be quite receptive to Magellan's plan of sailing westward till he could arrive on the eastern side of the Spice Islands. Magellan in his turn pointed out the advantage of Spain getting control of a westward sea route, since it would in effect be "west" of the dividing line through the Atlantic and thus in keeping with the Treaty of Tordesillas. On March 22, 1518, Magellan was finally granted a large sum of money by King Charles I which he used to gather a crew of 270 men and prepare five ships named the Conception, the San Antonio, the Santiago, the Trinidad, and the Victoria. Together they made up the Armada de Molluccas and Magellan took command of Trinidad. In September 1519, Magellan thus set sail westwards in search of a different route to the Spice Islands, during the course of which his ship would actually circle the globe.

The Voyage

The early part of the voyage was beset with problems. Because of his Portuguese origins, Magellan found it difficult to control his largely Spanish crew who began plotting against him. Fortunately for Magellan, these plans of mutiny could not be realized and he had several of the Spanish crew and officers either imprisoned or executed for rising against him. Then there were navigational problems since the ships were passing through Portuguese waters while he was sailing under the Spanish flag.

Several months of sailing westwards through the Atlantic Ocean brought them on the eastern coast of a continent which eventually came to be known as South America. The ships made landfall at the modern-day equivalent of Rio de Janeiro on December 13, 1519. This was a fortunate thing since the ships were running low on supplies and here Magellan was able to order the restocking of ships.

Thereafter, Magellan's ships set off again, sailing southwards along the eastern coast of the South American continent with the aim of looking for a route that would lead them into the Pacific Ocean. However, the weather began to turn for the worse and the ships were forced to dock at Port San Julian on the coast of today's equivalent of Patagonia so that they could wait out the harsh winter.

With the arrival of spring, the weather began to improve and Magellan once again became eager to search for the way into the Pacific Ocean. With this purpose, he sent a ship, the Santiago, westward but unfortunately it was shipwrecked during a fierce storm. Though the ship's crewmembers were rescued and were adjusted among the remaining ships, it was not before August that year, that Magellan could think of sailing again. Eventually after several months of difficult journey, the remaining four ships found a strait in October and proceeded to sail through it.

However, Magellan's troubles were still not at end. The journey through the strait not only took a long gruelling thirty-eight days but the crew of one of the ships, the San Antonio, abandoned the expedition and forced its captain to desert after which the ship turned and left for Spain. Together with the loss of a ship, Magellan also lost a huge amount of supplies. At long last in November 1520, Magellan and the remaining three ships were able to pass through the strait and cross over into the Pacific Ocean, thus paving the way for the first circumnavigation of the globe. In his gratitude and relief, Magellan named the passage the, Strait of All Saints.

The Pacific Ocean

By passing through the strait, Magellan and his crew became the first Europeans to cross into and behold the great ocean which he named Mar Pacifico or the Pacific Ocean. After the dangerous waters and rough weather of strait, the calm waters of this ocean impressed Magellan and thus he named it Pacifico which means peaceful. Ironically, though Pacific Ocean has long been the site of many storms, typhoons and tsunamis which have wreaked havoc on the Pacific Islands and Pacific Rim countries.

Since no one had traversed the mighty Pacific Ocean before, Magellan had no idea about the full expanse of the waters and mistakenly assumed that they would be able to reach the Spice Islands within a few weeks of their crossing the strait. Unfortunately, it would be an extremely arduous three-month voyage before Magellan's fleet would be able to touch land. This was a time of great hardship for Magellan and the crew – the provisions were running low and many among the crew had to go without food; some of the men developed diseases like scurvy and even the stored water turned putrid. In January 1521, the fleet came upon an island and the crew got some relief from hunger in the form of fish and sea-birds. However, the ship's provisions were still far from being adequately restocked and the fleet continued to sail in search of the Indies.

His Death

Finally, in March 28, 1521, Magellan's fleet arrived at the port of Guam where at last they replenished their store of food and water. On 28 March, the Armada landed on the island of Cebu which was part of the larger Philippines archipelago. Here Magellan befriended the local king named Raja Humabon and in return for the hospitality that he and his crew received, was persuaded to fight on behalf of the king against another a rival king, Lapu Lapu who was the chief of the neighbouring island of Mactan. Part of the reason why Magellan decided to take up arms was his sudden zeal in converting the local populace to Christianity and partly he was overconfident about the supposed superiority of European weapons; so even against the better judgement of his crew, Magellan went into the Battle of Mactan but was unfortunately killed by a poisoned arrow shot by Lapu Lapu's soldiers on April 21, 1521.

Magellan's Legacy

After Magellan's death, Sebastian del Cano took over the command of the fleet and crew members. Upon Sebastian's orders, the ship named Conception was burned so that the local enemies would not be able to use it against them. Out of the remaining two ships, one named the Trinidad was ordered to turn back and return to Spain while the other named Victoria continued on its westward journey. The Trinidad was unfortunately captured by Spain's arch-rival, Portugal as it tried to negotiate the complex waters without the expertise of Magellan's navigation. However, Victoria, pushing westward through the waters of Pacific and Indian Ocean and finally managed to find its way back to Spain. Though only one of the five original ships and a meagre crew of 18 men remained, Magellan's expedition had at last successfully circumnavigated the globe. And despite the fact that Magellan did not live to see his theory proved correct, he is hailed as the first person to circle the earth by sea since the expedition was his brainchild and for the most difficult part of the voyage, sailed under his command.

Braving through the uncharted waters on the eastern coast of South America, Magellan was also the first to cross the strait at the southern tip which eventually came to be named after him as the Strait of Magellan; consequently his was also the first expedition that entered the Pacific Ocean from the eastern part of South America and from where he could with great difficulty make for the South Asian Islands.

The full extent of Magellan's legacy can be gauged from the fact that an astronomical feature has also been named after the great explorer. The Magellanic Clouds are actually two irregular dwarf galaxies visible on the sky only from the southern hemisphere and perhaps because he was the first explorer to traverse the oceans in the southern hemisphere, the mini-galaxies today bear his name.

However, the most important contribution of Magellan to the history of human exploration remains the fact that his expedition proved the full extent of the vastness of the earth. He found not only a massive ocean, that was still unknown to Europeans at the time, but he also discovered that the earth was much larger than previously thought. And lastly though by the 15th century, it was accepted that the earth was not flat, Magellan's circumnavigation put to rest any further speculation on the matter and empirically proved that the earth was round.

□

9

Amerigo Vespucci

(1454-1512)

Amerigo Vespucci is today primarily remembered as the explorer who lent his name to two of the largest continents on the globe. Though it has become clearer in recent times, that there were not only Europeans who had visited the continents before him but there were actually indigenous people living there for centuries before the fifteenth century Spaniards came, still Vespucci continues to stand tall among the greatest explorers of the Age of Discovery.

Origins in Italy

Born in 1454 into a wealthy family of silk traders, Amerigo Vespucci was the son of a notary and lucky to be brought up in the cosmopolitan city of Florence, Italy. Knowledge was not difficult to acquire in this hub of Italian Renaissance and his uncle Giorgio Antonio saw to it that the young Vespucci was given a humanistic education. Soon Vespucci grew up to be a young man interested in books and maps with a strong entrepreneurial streak of personality.

In 1479, Vespucci was sent by the powerful Medici family of Italy to be their spokesman to the king of France. The Medicis must have been pleased with Vespucci's performance since after his return to Florence, the young man was taken into the banking sector controlled by Lorenzo and Giovanni di Pierfrancesco de' Medici.

Through his association with the Medicis, Vespucci in around 1491 came into contact with their agent Giannotto Berardi who had a side business of sorts, fitting out ships for long voyages. It is quite likely that Berardi was also known to the greatest explorers in Spain of the time and may have worked for Christopher Columbus too. Soon enough Vespucci landed in Spain which was fast becoming the hub of exploration endeavours to the New World, and in all likelihood he may have been there when Christopher Columbus returned from his first voyage. Through Berardi, Vespucci acquired first-hand knowledge about preparations for voyages and after the former's death in either late 1495 or early 1496, Vespucci was made the new manager of the Seville agency.

Staying in Seville around that time and probably having met Columbus too, Vespucci felt a burning ambition to follow his heart's desire which was to set out for the newly discovered lands westwards. He wanted to see these places with his own eyes and step on the very soil whose discovery had sent ripples through the court at Spain and elsewhere in Europe. The decision to set sail on a voyage was further aided by the fact that Vespucci's business which he had taken from Berardi was not doing well. Well into his 40s, Vespucci arrived at the decision that this was the time to leave the past behind and follow his dreams out into the oceans while he still could.

Vespucci and His Expeditions

There has been a great deal of debate about the exact number of voyages that Vespucci went on during his lifetime to the unexplored lands which lay west of the Atlantic Ocean. Two main sources have been available to historians about Vespucci's voyages – one is a letter in Italian written by the name of Vespucci and dated from Lisbon, Portugal, September 4, 1504 to some official named Piero Soderini, and which later came to be printed in Florence in 1505. The other source is a series of three private letters addressed to individuals of the Medici family. Unfortunately, there is a disparity in the number of voyages mentioned in the two sources and historians are yet to reconcile the two but so much is agreed that Vespucci undertook the main voyages between 1499 and 1504.

The First Major Voyage

In the first major voyage taken around 1499-1500, Vespucci was probably little more than a navigator. Even then he found himself in the company of such renowned explorers such as Alonso de Ojeda who had been present in Columbus's second voyage as well the famous cartographer of the time, Juan de la Cosa who had again served under Columbus on the latter's voyages. Among the chief successes of this expedition was the arrival at the mouth of the mighty Amazon River and exploration of much of the north-eastern coast of present-day South America. It is possible that Vespucci went as far south as Cape St. Augustine which bears the latitude about 6° S. On the way back, he came upon Trinidad and even discovered the mouth of the Orinoco River, after which he sailed towards Haiti. One of the lasting effects of this trip was the naming of a calm bay as Venezuela which translated as, 'Little Venice'.

At the time, Spanish explorers sailing westwards believed that the first major lands they would come across were bound to be a part of Asia. This was based on the newly-affirmed knowledge that the earth was a sphere and hence offered a way of reaching Asia other than by Africa and Persia. However, the explorers were not yet aware that the continents now known as the Americas existed in-between Europe and extreme eastern Asia. Thus, Christopher Columbus's arrival on the Bahamas was thought of as his discovery of the Indies and in keeping with the view, Vespucci too thought that he had sailed along the coast of the extreme easterly peninsula of Asia, where the ancient geographer Ptolemy, believed the market of Cattigara was located. Thus, Vespucci too searched for the tip of this peninsula, calling it Cape Cattigara. He assumed once the ships crossed this Cape, they would come upon the seas of southern Asia.

The Second Major Voyage

On the strength of his assumptions, Vespucci made a strong appeal to the Spanish Crown to fund another voyage so that he was able to cross the assumed Cape and access the Indian Ocean. However, no interest was shown in his plans and frustrated, Vespucci migrated to Portugal.

Vespucci seemed to have better luck with the Portuguese authorities with the result that on May 13, 1501 he was able to sail for his next expedition from Lisbon under the flag of Portugal. With a brief stop at Cape Verde, Vespucci sailed in a south-westerly direction until he touched Cape St. Augustine on the coast of Brazil. Owing to favourable winds, it had taken Vespucci's fleet only 64 days to cross the Atlantic and reach South America.

Over the course of this voyage, Vespucci and the ships traced practically the entire length of the South American coast. It is likely that during this time Vespucci came in view of Guanabara Bay which marks present-day Rio de Janeiro's bay and sailed as far as the Río de la Plata, making Vespucci the first European to discover that estuary. According to other accounts, he may have travelled till 400 miles short of Tierra del Fuego which marks the southern tip of the continent.

Not much is known about Vespucci's return voyage to Portugal, though it is on record that he docked at the Port of Lisbon on July 22, 1502. As far as his legacy is concerned, this voyage was also the most significant since this confirmed his suspicion that the islands and mainland lying to the west of the Atlantic Ocean was not Asia but a new landmass entirely, soon to be hailed as the New World.

The success of his 1501 voyage cemented Vespucci's position as one of the foremost explorers of the day and he was made the Pilot Major of Spain in 1508. This put him in-charge of the planning and co-ordination of Spanish explorations to the West Indies and the rest of the New World. To a great extent, Vespucci's popularity back in Europe owed to the large circulation of letters that he sent home from his voyages. These letters not only affirmed his stance the West Indies was a New World, different from Asia, but also described the new cultures and their practices over the course of his travels.

His Later Years

It is likely that Vespucci set off on another voyage in his later years, sometime 1503-04. This expedition was probably directly commissioned by the Portuguese government and he was accompanied by a renowned explorer of Portugal, Gonzalo Coelho. There are contradicting reports about what was achieved on this – according to some historians, nothing new of value was discovered while some believe that towards the end of the voyage, Vespucci came upon Bahia and the Island of South Georgia. In any case, the expedition was cut short by the non-cooperation of the captains of other ships and, in 1504, he returned to Lisbon.

Though Vespucci may not have been out at sea at this time, he was still respected as one of the most renowned explorers of this age – so much so that in early 1505, the Court of Spain offered him an exalted office at the newly-founded Commercial House for the Indies or *Casa de Contratación de las Indias.* In 1508, he was appointed as chief navigator of Spain – a highly coveted post since it was responsible for evaluating the capabilities of pilots and masters of the ships before they were given licenses for voyages. This appointment also put him in-charge of a new school of navigation, set up to standardize navigation procedures and practices used by ships across Europe. Most importantly as the chief navigator, Vespucci was in-charge of preparing the official map of newly discovered lands and the routes by which they could be reached. The new maps would eventually be used for royal survey and for the purpose Vespucci had to coordinate and evaluate all data given by the captains of ships returning from various voyages. In 1512, he contracted malaria and died in Spain at the age of 58.

Vespucci's Legacy

Vespucci's reputation has gone through wild extremes – while at one time he held the most prestigious offices in Spain, centuries later he has been viewed as a fraud who tried to steal from Columbus, the credit of 'discovering' America.

The truth is that it was never Vespucci's own idea to get the two new-found continents named after him. Among those most impressed by the written account of Vespucci's travels was Martin Waldseemüller, a German scholar and clergyman. At the time Waldseemüller was working on a world map and in his enthusiasm to come up with the latest version, he quickly named the newly discovered landmass after Vespucci's Christian name as he believed that the Florentine was the true discoverer of the New World. Even after Waldseemüller later realized his mistake and tried to set things right, the new name for the continents, 'America', stuck and quickly began to be used by other cartographers of Europe. In 1538, a map-maker named Gerardus Mercator used the name, 'America' to designate both the northern and southern landmasses of the New World, and the continents have been known as such ever since. Fortunately, the real discoverer of the New World, Christopher Columbus, is believed to have accepted the turn of events with good grace and never seemed to have objected to the mistaken credit lauded on Vespucci, though till the end of his life Columbus privately clung to his belief that the shores he had landed on were indeed that of India.

In the end, the chief contribution of Vespucci to the history of human exploration lies in the fact that he identified the Americas as a distinct landmass; he realized that Columbus's arrival on the shores of West Indies had not really found a new route to Asia but heralded the European discovery of an entirely new land altogether. Even more significantly Vespucci was the first person to recognize North and South America as distinct continents that were previously unknown to the world. Thus today, Vespucci's legacy seems to be the identification of the New World and it seems only fitting that the continents bear his name.

□

10

Vasco da Gama

(1460-1524)

Vasco da Gama is today chiefly known as the explorer who found a direct sea route from Europe to India. With the discovery of the eastward sea route, he not only came up with a faster path to the lucrative markets of the East but also paved the way for large-scale interaction between the two continents of Europe and Asia.

The Geo-political Context

The stupendous advances made by European explorers in the 15th and 16th centuries marked the Age of Discovery. Traders and navigators around this time were keen to find routes to Asian lands that were famous for precious goods such as spices, silk, gold and gemstones. Though there was a land route from Europe to Asia, primarily the Silk Road, the rough terrain and harsh climate of the way made this an extremely hazardous journey. And this is why explorers were keen to come up with a sea route that would cut down on the time and dangers of the way to Asia.

At the time, Portugal had established itself as a formidable seafaring nation. Much of the credit for this goes to a figure of remarkable intelligence and far-sightedness from the Portuguese royal family, Prince Henry the Navigator. Based in the southern part of the country, Henry's haunt quickly became the nerve centre of the latest technological developments in the field of nautical navigation and exploration. His team consisted of brilliant navigators, map-makers and sea-men of the time and he even sent out expeditions to explore the western coast of Africa so that Portugal's commercial influence could be extended. At that time, trade with Africa was mainly based on gold and slavery but slowly the Portuguese royals realized that real money lay in the spices for which they became eager to get a foothold into the highly lucrative spice trade between Europe and Asia.

Though the western coast of Africa had been explored by Portuguese sailors and merchants, the southern and eastern portions of the continent continued a mystery till one man managed to reach till the southern tip and rounded the Cape that existed there. This was Bartolomeu Dias – a brave and intelligent navigator whose voyage around the Cape proved, for the first time, that one could travel from the Atlantic Ocean into the Indian Ocean. The consequences for geographic exploration were also significant since the discovery motivated navigators to look for a new eastwards trade route to India by sea.

Early Life

Biographical details from the early life of Vasco da Gama are rather sketchy; he was born sometime around 1460 to a minor Portuguese official whose job was to command the fortress at Sines, located in south-western Portugal on the coast of the Alentejo province.

At the time, the competition between European countries for control of trading rights and routes was becoming increasingly fierce. Nations like Portugal, Spain, France and England were often at odds with each other, either overtly or covertly for to gain an upper hand in trade with the Orient. So when in 1492 the French forces launched an attack on Portuguese ships, King John II of Portugal sought retaliation against the French and for the purpose sent da Gama to the port city of Setubal located on the south of Lisbon. This was one of the first instances where Vasco da Gama found himself in the midst of action and proved himself a capable soldier.

However, da Gama's heart lay in venturing forth on the seas. When King John II was succeeded by King Manuel I, da Gama's dream came further closer to reality. At that time, European traders not only had to encounter the hazards of overland journey to reach Asia but they also had to contend with Muslim intermediaries who controlled trade with precious Oriental products, particularly, the spices of southern India. Like the rulers of other nations, the Portuguese king was also in search of alternative routes to India which would bypass the Muslim middlemen of Africa and Middle East. By the late 1490s, however, King Manuel was not only concerned about commercial opportunities as he set his sights on the East – in fact a growing reason for the quest was the desire to conquer Islam and establish himself as the king of Jerusalem. Eventually, King Manuel I decided that Vasco da Gama would lead a Portuguese expedition to India in search of a maritime route from western Europe to the East.

The First Voyage

In July 1497, Vasco da Gama sailed from Lisbon with his fleet which consisted of four ships, including his flagship, the 200-ton St. Gabriel, and a crew of 170 men. Initially, they sailed in a southward direction, keeping close to the coast of Africa; however eager to avoid contrary currents, da Gama mistakenly sailed into the waters of southern Atlantic. Eventually, after a great deal of difficulty, he was able to navigate the expedition around the southern tip of the African continent and emerge onto the eastern coast. This southern tip had been so often the site of shipwrecks that after it had come to be named as Cape of Good Hope, in an attempt to keep the crews from despairing.

After crossing the Cape, da Gama's expedition turned north, hugging Africa's eastern coast, and stopped at important port cities like Mozambique, Mombasa and Malindi – the last two of which now form part of modern Kenya. Eventually, da Gama was able to secure the help of an experienced guide who helped to navigate the expedition eastwards. At last in May 1497, almost a full year after setting out from Lisbon, Vasco da Gama touched the shores of Calicut, one of the busiest ports on the coast of south-western India, which is now known as Kozhikode.

Initially, the local population welcomed the Portuguese expedition. However, when their king saw that the foreign traders had come bearing rather modest gifts but in exchange wanted major trading concessions, ties became strained. To add to the confusion, da Gama mistook the local people for Christians – the people were actually Hindus, a religion that da Gama and his crew had never heard of. The local Muslim traders too fanned the simmering dissatisfaction since they were unhappy at the loss of their monopoly in trading with Indian spices and other precious goods. In fact, things came to such a pass that da Gama and his crew were not even allowed into the city and were forced to barter on the waterfront just to acquire enough goods for the passage home. Soon enough the discontent erupted into a full-scale conflict and da Gama to leave hastily.

In August 1498, da Gama and his men began their return voyage back to Portugal but they continued to face problems on the day. Their return voyage coincided with the onset of monsoons over the Indian Ocean and the fleet suffered from fierce storms. In an effort to economize his fleet, da Gama even had to order the burning of one of his ships.

Finally in July 1499, da Gama arrived at Lisbon – he had spent almost three hundred days at sea and travelled nearly 24,000 miles which was a major feat even for the enthusiastic explorers of the time. And yet his first voyage to India was not without its costs. He had been compelled to leave Calicut in haste without concluding any treaty with the king there. Also he had been away from home for nearly two years and the voyage had cost the lives of several of his men – from the original crew of 170 men only 54 made it back to Lisbon, many of them succumbing to hunger, thirst and diseases such as scurvy; in fact, da Gama's brother Bartholomeo was among those who could to survive the voyage back to Europe.

Consequences of the First Voyage

Though Vasco da Gama's path-breaking voyage to India had cost him men, its success in terms of commercial advantage and nautical exploration was immense. Once having discovered a direct sea route, Portugal was now determined to establish its control of the route. Also Portugal was keen to push its own trading activities in Calicut and for the purpose planned to sent a force to quell the influence of the Muslim traders as well as secure a trading post at Calicut. For the purpose, a larger fleet than da Gama's first one was sent to India under the command of Pedro Álvares Cabral. Thanks to da Gama's discovery of the direct route, the crew reached India in just six months.

A conflict between the newly-arrived Portuguese forces and the longtime Muslim traders was now inevitable. So when the latter killed 50 of Cabral's men, the Portuguese commander struck back by burning 10 Muslim cargo vessels and killing nearly 600 sailors aboard. He then headed for Cochin, another important port city on India's south-western coast, and set up Portugal's first trading post in India.

Back at home, Vasco da Gama was decorated with many awards and titles. He received the noble title of Dom and was allowed to use it for himself, his siblings and their descendants. Even more impressive was the title of "Admiral of the Seas of Arabia, Persia, India and all the Orient", with which he was decorated on 30 January 1502. Also after his return to Lisbon, he got married to a woman from a reputed family. His wife, Catarina de Ataíde, was the daughter of Álvaro de Ataíde, a well-known nobleman and a relation of powerful Almeida family of Portugal. da Gama would go on to have six sons with Catarina.

The Second Voyage

In 1502, Vasco da Gama was given the charge of heading another expedition to India by King Manuel I who by this time had become obsessed with enforcing Portuguese religious and commercial control, by force if necessary. Armed with a large fleet of twenty ships, thus Vasco da Gama set sail in February that year.

He initially stopped at the eastern coast of Africa where he unleashed one of the most brutal attacks of the Age of Discovery. Local Muslim ports, trading centres and ships were destroyed by Portuguese soldiers and it is believed even a ship returning from a pilgrimage in Mecca containing women and children was not spared.

Vasco da Gama then turned his attention eastwards. After reaching India, he launched a concerted offensive upon the Muslim traders of Calicut and nearby trading communities. It is believed that da Gama's men destroyed the city's main trading port and killed 38 hostages. From Calicut, Vasco da Gama next moved further south to the city of Cochin where he terrorized the local ruler into signing a treaty that was heavily in favour of Portuguese interests.

With significant military and commercial victories to his credit this time, Vasco da Gama and his crew finally left for home on February 20, 1503 and arrived at Portugal on October 11 of that year. On his return journey, Vasco da Gama established Portuguese trading posts along the eastern coast of Africa, especially in what is now Mozambique. Though the spice trade would prove to be a major asset to the Portuguese royal treasury, da Gama's voyage had also made it clear that the east coast of Africa, the Contra Costa, too had to be brought under control in order to protect Portuguese trading interests. The ports of eastern Africa were essential to provide fresh water, provisions, timber, and harbours for repairs of trading fleets. Also they served as a refuge where ships could wait out unfavourable weather in the Indian Ocean. Eventually, the city of Mozambique would emerge as one of the biggest strongholds of Portuguese colonial power.

Later Life

Having returned to Portugal from his second voyage, Vasco da Gama settled down to a quiet family life. For twenty odd years, he remained distant from the royal court and the hub of colonial exploration and politics. A new group of noblemen was now in favour with King Manuel I and they comprised of powerful figures such as Afonso de Albuquerque, Almeida, and later Sequeira and Albergaria who now advised the Portuguese Emperor on colonial matters, especially those related to India.

However in 1519, King Manuel I relented a little and awarded a feudal title to Vasco da Gama, making him the First Count of Vidigueira. With this title, Vasco da Gama became the first Portuguese count who was not born with royal blood.

After the death of King Manuel I in late 1521, his son and successor, King John III was determined to break the grip of Albuquerque and his favourites on the strategic policies of Portugal. Hence, the new king brought back Vasco da Gama to the royal court and made the aging explorer the adviser on colonial matters. da Gama warned King John II of Spain's expanding influence on the Malacca Islands and advised him to focus on Portuguese territories in India rather than those of Africa.

The fact that Menezes, who had been left in India as the Governor, had ruined Portuguese prospects with rampant corruption and inefficiency also worked in da Gama's favour. Hence, in February 1524, John III granted Vasco da Gama the highly-prized title of 'Viceroy' and gave him permission to govern Portuguese interests in India. Three months later, in April 1524, Vasco da Gama along with two of his sons, Estevao and Paulo, set sail with a fleet of fourteen ships, taking as his flagship the famous large carrack Santa Catarina do Monte Sinai on its last journey to India. However, soon after his arrival in India, the aging da Gama came down with malaria and died on Christmas Eve in 1524. His body was buried for sometime at St. Francis Church in the city of Cochin; eventually in 1539, his remains were returned to Portugal.

Legacy of Vasco da Gama

For long Vasco da Gama was hailed as the man who paved the way for Europe's commercial and political ascendency over the Orient. However, now as the full cost of European colonization to the subjugated countries becomes clearer and the darkest stories of colonial force emerge, the legacy of Vasco da Gama has come under some qualification. Nevertheless, the Portuguese explorer remains one of the foremost figures of the history of human exploration – no matter what his personal fallacies were, so much remains without a doubt that the direct sea route to India that Vasco da Gama discovered went on to make significant additions to the map of the world and eventually determined the course of world history.

At the same time, for better or worse, da Gama placed Portugal in a prominent position in Indian Ocean trade and ensured that the country's colonial and commercial assets were one of the most extensive in the world – a feat that came to be amply celebrated in Portugal's national epic, *The Lusiads*, composed by the country's greatest poet Luis de Camoes. As a mark of the highest honour to its explorer son, Portugal in 1880, decided to move the remains of Vasco da Gama along with the poet Camoes to new carved tombs in the nave of the church of the Hieronymites Monastery located in the Belem area of Lisbon. This is only a few meters away from the tombs of the kings Manuel I and John III whom Gama had served and thus is a marker of the high regard given to Vasco da Gama by his country.

□

11

Sir Francis Drake

(C. 1540-1596)

While countries like Spain and Portugal had a headstart in maritime exploration, coming across new lands which people in Europe knew nothing about, England did not take long to catch up. And the remarkable thing about the greatest English explorers of the times is that they came from all kinds of social groups. Though noblemen had the easiest access to scientific education and hence became expert navigators and explorers, there were some who though belonging to dubious social groups like pirates – through action and ambition – performed amazing feats of exploration and were rewarded with fame and success. And one of the names which belong to the latter group is that of swashbuckling Elizabethan hero, Sir Francis Drake, who became famous for this voyage round the world as well as for his role in the defeat of the Spanish Armada.

Early Life

Like much about Francis Drake's life, the exact date of his birth also seems a mystery. In those times, birth records rarely existed for people belonging to humble backgrounds. Historians based on dates of later events now believe that he was born sometime between 1540 and 1544. There is however a record of his first command of a ship in 1566 when his age was given as 22. Then again there are two portraits which further narrow the date of his birth; one of these was painted in 1581, when he was 42, and the other was done in 1594, when he was 53. Thus, the safest date Francis Drake's birth seems to be sometime around 1540.

The eldest of a twelve children, Francis Drake was born to Edmund Drake and Mary Mylwaye Drake. Edmund was a farmer on the estate of Lord Francis Russell, the second earl of Bedford. However, owing to certain developments, sometime in the 1550s Edmund had to leave Tavistock with his family and move to Kent, nearer the sea. There the family lived in the hulk of an old ship as Edmund scraped a living preaching the word of God to the sailors of the navy. In this way, young Francis started living among seamen, hearing their yarns and learning about ships which would pave the way for his later maritime involvement. Soon enough, Francis was apprenticed to a merchant who often sailed between England and France for the purpose of trading goods. The boy quickly took to the life at sea and must have some personal charm too as the old captain, having no family of his own, left the ship to Drake in his will.

Life as a Privateer

As Francis Drake proved his seaworthiness, soon enough, he came into the notice of his extended family members, the Hawkinses. They were privateers or pirates who sometimes came to the aid of the Crown seizing enemy ships or goods and received a share of the loot. The Hawkins family especially focused on the shipping lanes off the French coast, raiding merchant ships.

Though maritime trade in exotic goods was still lucrative, a new trade was fast coming up in the wake of increasing discovery of new lands and their colonization. This was the slave trade according to which the men, women and even children would be bought or abducted from Africa and sold to settlers in different parts of the world, especially the new colonies in the Americas.

By the 1560s, Francis Drake had gathered sufficient knowledge and resources to be able to command of his own ship, the Judith. Then Drake and his cousin, John Hawkins, got together a small fleet with the intention of sailing to Africa to engage in the slave trade. Once they had got the captives, they then headed to New Spain to sell the slaves to the settlers. However, slave trade was illegal under Spanish law and when in 1568, Drake and Hawkins were docked at the Mexican Port of San Juan de Ulua, the Spanish forces launched a scathing attack on the slave traders. Though Hawkins and Drake managed to escape, many of their men lost their lives in the skirmish. This incident left Drake with a deep-hatred for the Spanish forces as well as their increasing influence on colonial trade.

In 1569, after his return to England from the ill-fated voyage, Drake married Mary Newman. At that time, he was still a relatively unknown young sailor and similarly little is known about Mary too. The couple had no children and she died twelve years later, leaving the then-newly knighted Sir Francis Drake a widower.

In the meantime, Francis Drake received a privateer's commission from Queen Elizabeth I in 1572. This gave him the license to attack and loot any of the ships sailing under the flag of King Philip of Spain. Armed with the commission, Francis Drake set off for his first independent voyage to Panama where he planned to attack the town of Nombre Dios. This was famous as a destination of the Spanish ships which would drop off their cargo of gold and silver that they were bringing from Peru. Armed with two ships and a crew of 73 men, Drake seized Nombre Dios but was badly injured in the ensuing fight and had to lie low till his wounds healed. After his recuperation though, Drake launched a series of attacks on the Spanish-held towns of Panama coast, looting reserves of gold and silver. Laden with all the booty, Francis Drake came back to Plymouth in 1573.

Starting for the Voyage

As news of Francis Drake's successful attack on the Spanish settlements in Panama as well as the size of loot reached the Queen's ears, she decided to send him on an even more daring journey. She ordered Drake to sail along the Pacific Coast of South America and unleash whatever damage he could upon the Spanish settlers there. Accordingly, Drake set off in 1577 in the company of two other privateers, John Wynter and Thomas Doughty. The three agreed to share the responsibilities as well as the rewards of command equally through the expedition. The fleet consisted of five ships and Drake sailed in his flagship, The Pelican.

The expedition was shrouded in mystery even before it had begun. To all it was declared as a trading expedition to the Nile but upon reaching Africa, the true destination was revealed to be the Pacific Ocean via the Strait of Magellan. Not surprisingly, this created discontent among many of the officers and men of the crew. Anyway, the expedition first sailed to the Azores and plundered Spanish settlements there. However, with Drake taking over the command of the expedition, Doughty was left miffed. The conflicts between Drake and Doughty continued to escalate all the way across the Atlantic till upon their arrival in Argentina, Drake had Doughty arrested on suspicions that the latter was planning a mutiny. After a quick trial whose validity was somewhat questionable, Doughty was convicted and executed. Thereupon Drake took full command of the expedition and ensured that all officers and crew were not directly and only answerable to him. As a symbolic gesture of his new authority, Drake now renamed his flagship, The Golden Hind.

Journey along the South American Coast

In September 1578, the fleet, now consisting of three ships, headed into one of the most difficult parts of the voyage, the Strait of Magellan. This region was infamous among sailors as the site of terrible Pacific storms which had wreaked havoc on many an expedition. For two months, Drake's ships too were in serious danger – trapped in a stormy region, they were able neither to sail clear of the weather, not to stay clear of the coast. Battered by the never-ending storms, the ships of the fleet got scattered. While the smallest, the Marigold, was lost to the sea, the Elizabeth commanded by John Wynter turned up on the Strait and soon decided to go back to England, where she arrived safely but in disgrace. Meanwhile, the Golden Hind had been blown far to the south and one of the results was the discovery for Drake of the existence of open water below the South American continent, as opposed to the conventional thought that the southern tip of the continent marked the end of the globe.

Once Drake was able to get the bearings of his ships, he launched into a northward course, sailing along the western coast of South America. They first stopped at the now Chilean Island of Mocha where provisions of food and water were restocked. Next Drake sailed onto raid the Spanish settlements all along the western coast of their wealth of gold and silver which the Spanish in turn had looted from the indigenous people. Among the Spanish settlements which suffered the brunt of Drake's fury were the Valpariso, Lima and Arica in the regions which now constitute Peru and Chile. The largely unprotected Spanish ships fell easily to Drake's forces and one of the biggest catch was the large treasure ship Cacafuego, which had gold, silver and other precious goods as its cargo. The onslaught by Drake's men on the Spanish ships and port towns of the western coast continued for at least five months and left panic, destruction and intense Spanish outrage in its wake. However, according to some sources, the plundering was largely devoid of casualties – both Spanish settlers and the indigenous population were on the whole left unharmed. To add to the element of chaos, no one was sure how many men Drake had under his command and there were reports wildly ranging from sixty to more than a hundred.

Reaching the western coast of present-day Mexico, Drake's ship stopped for repairs at the island of Cano. After a final raid on the nearby town of Guatulco which no longer exists on the map, the, Golden Hind, sailed out of Spanish waters. By this time, Drake had amassed a massive fortune on his ship with some sources putting the figures of the plunder to twenty-six tons of silver.

Arriving at North America

Next Drake ordered his ship to sail in a westerly direction and then turn north which brought him along the western coast of the continent of Northern America. Here he stopped at an area – which corresponds roughly with the coast of California – to carry out repairs on his damaged ship and restock provisions. He named the region, New Albion, and took possession of it in the name of Queen Elizabeth-I, even though the Spanish had most likely already visited it and named it in their maps.

The northernmost point that, Golden Hind, reached has been a matter of a great deal of debate. It is variously reported as 48 degrees and 42 degrees north latitude but the question is further complicated by his descriptions of places with snow-covered mountains even at the peak and people dressed in clothing that resembles Native American tribes living farther north, even perhaps on the Canadian coast. In one of the descriptions of a period of encampment, Drake talks of the people of New Albion living in low, wood-pole structures covered with earth and a vent on top. Apart from this, there are accounts of indigenous people leading a markedly maritime culture as well as their skill with bow and arrow for hunting.

After making sure his ship was fully sea-worthy and its larder was stocked with provisions, Drake headed out west into the Pacific Ocean. Next Drake entered the Indonesian archipelago and his passage through the hundreds of Islands here was extremely lucrative. In the beginning, at least he was able to make profitable transactions, buying spices in large quantities and entering into favourable alliance with local rulers. However, in January 1580, the Golden Hind, began facing problems in finding its way about the numerous islands and then accidently ran onto a reef. It was only after several days of panic-stricken wait, that a change of wind put the ship back on its course.

Return to England

Sailing westward, Drake crossed the Indian Ocean without any mishap. After passing around the Cape of Good Hope, the expedition once again entered the Atlantic and after travelling up western coast of Africa, finally arrived in England in the autumn of 1580. Drake and his crew had thus been on the voyage for around three years and crossed some 36,000 miles becoming the first

Englishmen and the second expedition after Magellan's, to circumnavigate the globe.

Drake's return into England was marked by a shower of royal praise and financial rewards. In 1581, the Queen knighted him and later that year, he was elected to the House of Commons. Then there was the immense treasure he had compiled during the voyage and all this made him a very wealthy man as well as the object of adulation from various quarters. In 1585, Drake married Elizabeth Sydenham, a woman from a rich, well-connected family who was around twenty years younger to him. The couple moved into Buckland Abbey that Drake had newly purchased and which even now houses many of his artefacts. However like with Mary Newman, this marriage of Drake too did not yield any children.

Defeat of the Spanish Armada

Increasing rivalry between Spain and England over shipping routes and colonial trade during 1585-86 prompted Queen Elizabeth-I to order Sir Francis Drake back to the sea. In a series of lightning quick raids, Drake seized several cities in North and South America that were under Spanish control. Spain was left not only smarting from damaged pride but loss of huge amounts of treasure. King Phillip of Spain retaliated by raising a huge fleet of warships equipped with the latest weaponry and large enough to take on huge armies – this became the famous Spanish Armada.

Sir Francis Drake though, true to his swashbuckling style, launched a pre-emptive strike on the Spanish city of Cadiz, which resulted in the destruction of at least 30 ships for Spain and loss of thousands of tons of supplies. The incident was apparently referred to as, "singing the king of Spain's beard," by Drake who quickly grew into a national hero and one of the Queen's personal favourites. She rewarded him with the appointment of the Vice-Admiral of the English Navy in 1588.

In the meanwhile, on 21 July, 130 ships of the Spanish Armada sailed, in a crescent formation, into the English Channel. The Admiral, Lord John Howard and Sir Francis Drake decided to play up the English fleet's advantage of smaller, quicker boats. For several days, the English boats continued to ambush the Spanish fleet. Gradually, the Spanish morale began to sink as the losses piled up. Apart from damaging two Spanish ships, the English were able to capture one of the Spanish ships carrying the payroll for the Spanish Army. On July 27, a stealthy overnight English attack caught the Spanish by surprise and forced them to scatter.

Now with the Armada formation broken, the clumsy Spanish galleons were easy targets for the English ships, which were smaller, speedier and more manoeuvrable. The final damage was inflicted by weather as the fleeing Spanish ships were driven away from the Scottish shore and hurled onto Irish rocks by a strong gale. In the end, of the 25,000 Spanish soldiers that had set out in the Armada, less than 10,000 were able to go back home with their lives intact.

Later Expeditions and Death

With Sir Francis Drake's reputation as the conqueror of the Spanish Armada, he was again ordered by Queen Elizabeth in 1589 to leave on an expedition to destroy any remaining Spanish ships from the original fleet. Drake was also required to head to Lisbon where the English were planning to aid the Portuguese who were rising in rebellion against Spanish forces.

However, this expedition was singularly unsuccessful. Drake not only lost twenty of ships to the Spanish but as many as twelve thousand men of the English crew lost their lives. Eventually, Drake returned to England and for a while devoted himself to his duties as a Mayor of Plymouth.

Queen Elizabeth summoned Sir Francis Drake again in 1595 and sent him to an expedition against the Spanish for what was to prove the last time. The destination was Panama where the English forces were to seize all the treasure and in the process, deal a crushing blow to the Spain's main source of revenue. Aboard his flagship Defiance, Drake set sail with his cousin, Sir John Hawkins and at the beginning the English were able to main scattered gains in the Caribbean. From there the expedition sailed for Panama and anchored off the coast of Portobello. Here he contracted a tropical illness and soon became gravely ill. According to some anecdotes, on January 28, in the pre-dawn hours, Drake rose from his sickbed with the intention of putting on his armour so that he could die as a soldier. After his death, he was buried at sea off Portobello, Panama, in a lead coffin.

His Legacy

Though Sir Francis Drake started out as a slave trader and privateer, he eventually went on to become one of the most famous public figures of England. His description of the circumnavigation of the globe remains one of the best loved stories of the sea in his country. He was not only the first English to command a voyage circling the globe but also a shrewd and daring warrior who played a pivotal role in England's victory over the Spanish Armada. The feats of Sir Francis Drake bolstered English pride and ensured that England was a force to reckon with in the race for expanding colonies around the world.

□

12

Sir Walter Raleigh

(1552-1618)

The reign of Queen Elizabeth I in England is often upheld as a typical flowering of the fruits of Renaissance – not only was she surrounded by the finest poets, dramatists and intellectuals but she was paid homage by the most brilliant courtiers and explorers of the time. And one man who symbolized the multi-faceted character of the iconic Renaissance man was Sir Walter Raleigh. Apart from impressing the Queen with his chivalry, poetry and wit, he undertook many daring voyages into the new world and in the process, he established a colony near Roanoke Island, which he named Virginia, after his beloved Elizabeth I, known as the Virgin Queen.

Early Life

Typical of the times, no reliable records exist of Raleigh's birth as he came from a humble background. He was probably born sometime in 1552 in Devon, England. However, his parents had some kind of aristocratic lineage which is why young Raleigh managed to receive an education at Oriels College in Oxford when he was sixteen. Despite his modest beginning, Raleigh was a brilliant young man and quickly made favourites wherever he went. For a time he left his studies to go on a military expedition to France where he joined the Huguenot Army. After his return to England in around 1575, he completed his education in law.

In the Royal Court

As father had married three times, young Raleigh had several half-brothers, some of whom were already familiar faces in the Elizabethan courts. In 1578, it was decided that Raleigh would accompany his half-brother Sir Humphrey Gilbert, in 1578 when he led an expedition west to find the fabled Northwest Passage which was believed to offer a faster westwards route from Europe to Asia through the Arctic Circle. Not only such a proposition had to take into account of the harsh climate of the Arctic regions, but also the Spanish ships prowling the waters off the North American coasts; because of these potential problems, Gilbert's expedition never actually took off.

Instead Raleigh found himself heading for Ireland where at that time the English forces were trying to establish their dominance over Irish. Here Raleigh not only put down the Irish rebellion with fierce determination but even killed thousands of Spanish troops who had come down to support the traditionally catholic Irish. This was followed by the settlement of English and Scottish Protestants in Munster. The brute violence unleashed by Raleigh against the Irish and Spanish, especially at the Siege of Smerwick, raises many eyebrows today but at the time, the ferocity of his attacks against the Catholic rebels and soldiers earned him a foothold in the Elizabethan court. Thus, when he returned to London, he was able to use his stint in Ireland and his victory to secure a position of advisor in court on Irish Affairs.

One of the consequences of his entry into the court was that Raleigh came into the notice of Queen Elizabeth I. Using his quick wit and charm, Raleigh soon endeared himself to the Queen and according to popular accounts, even became her lover, though many authorities continue to doubt the historical accuracy of this lore. What is beyond any dispute however is that in the early to mid-1580s Raleigh was one of the most influential men in the Elizabethan court and definitely one of the Queen's most favourite courtiers. Elizabeth I had already rewarded him with a large estate in Ireland, and in 1585, she knighted him and rewarded him with trade privileges and the right to establish colonies in America.

The Colony of Virginia

Flush with increasing influence at court, Raleigh sent out a reconnaissance voyage in around 1584 led by Philip Amadas and Arthur Barlowe, which returned with gushing accounts of a fertile land and friendly on the shores of the newly-discovered continent of North America. Soon after Raleigh himself set out to explore the land from North Carolina to present-day Florida, and eventually named the region, Virginia, in honour of Elizabeth I who was known as the "virgin queen."

The Roanoke Experiment

However, not all ventures met with equal success. In 1585, Raleigh sent out around a hundred colonists in seven ships to establish a colony on Roanoke Island, off the coast of modern-day North Carolina. The expedition was led by Sir Richard Grenville and Sir Ralph Lane. The settlers constructed a fort, built several houses and planted crops for sustenance. They even searched for gold which according to popular myth, the colonies were teeming with.

However, within a year, it became clear that the colony was to be a failure. Not only the colonists could not take to the new place, but the hot and humid climate proved difficult to adjust to and the English settlers were especially terrified of the local weather phenomenon of hurricanes. Also the Native American tribes were far from happy about this intrusion onto their traditional space with the result that the settlers were involved in repeated skirmishes with indigenous people. The expedition thus proved to be a failure and soon returned to England. Even though the settlers ultimately left the place, this was the first Roanoke settlement in the history of the continent, and the first English colony in America.

According to some sources, Raleigh ordered the founding of a second colony in 1587. As part of this expedition, a British man named John White arrived in Roanoke in 1587 with more colonists. However, White decided to sail back to England after a few weeks so as to bring more provisions. At the time, England and Spain were engaged in constant battles at sea and this delayed White's return to the colony in North America. It was 1591 when he managed to land on the North American shore but as he arrived at the colony, he was not met by a single soul. It seemed that all the settlers had simply disappeared. There were no visible signs of violence or battle – only the word "Croatoan" was carved on the bark of a tree in the settlement. Even to this day, historians are puzzled about what actually happened in the settlement after White left. Theories about the missing colonists range from theories that they must have been killed by native American tribes to more vague suggestions that they must have migrated to live with the natives, or perhaps on nearby Croatoan island.

Back in England, Raleigh tried to offset the failure of the Roanoke experiment by throwing himself into military action at sea. In 1588, he joined the English ships in their fight against the Spanish armada and took part in the raids which brought victory to the English forces. Later Raleigh also set sail in search of Spanish ships carrying precious cargo from the colonies and much in the manner of a privateer, returned to England with all the fruits of plunder.

Falling Out of Royal Favour

Despite these intermittent successes, the failure of Raleigh's Roanoke expedition came to be, in a way, reflected in his personal affairs. In the early 1590s, Raleigh started courting one of the Queen's maids-in-waiting, Elizabeth Throckmorton and in 1592, he secretly married her too. When the news of Raleigh's marriage came to light, the Queen was furious at evidence of such disloyalty and had the couple imprisoned in the tower of London.

Though with the help of his charm and courtly finesse, Raleigh was able to gain the Queen's forgiveness and was eventually released from the tower, he soon realized that he had lost the royal favour forever.

Search for El Dorado

In a last desperate bid to amend things between him and the Queen, Raleigh decided to head off on an expedition to the New

World in search of the legendary El Dorado. He promised Elizabeth I that he would lavish all the gold of El Dorado at the Queen's feet, much like Spanish explorers like Cortez and Pizarro had done for the Spanish crown. Along with words of flattery, Raleigh also pointed out the need for prompt action so that the gold of El Dorado could be found before the Spanish by the Queen of England's representatives. This appeal to the Queen's desire to out-do the Spanish found its mark and Raleigh was granted the permission to try his luck in looking for the legendary city.

Though exaggerated by today's standards, it did not seem such an unlikely promise at that time. El Dorado was one of the most exciting and enduring myths to come out of the discovery of the New World. El Dorado was thought of as a lost city teeming with gold, silver and precious stones. Its reputation as the richest city in the world drew in hordes of expeditions from almost all seafaring European countries who just couldn't have enough of colonial treasures.

Though the legend of El Dorado may seem fantastical now, it appears that the myth was based on a sliver of truth. In ancient Colombia, the Muisca tribe had a tradition where their king would cover himself in gold dust and dive into Lake Guatavitá. In the earliest days of Spanish exploration of South America, their conquistadors came to hear this story and thus began the hunt for the kingdom of El Dorado which translates into Spanish as the 'gilded one'. Soon El Dorado came to be used interchangeably for the lost Peruvian city of Manoa, also thought to contain all the riches of ancient Inca tribes. Though some explorers later claimed to discover Lake Guatavita, upon dredging it, they found only a little gold at the bottom – not the proportions that was promised in the legend and hence the search for the legendary city of gold continued.

Based on the yarns of mariners and feats of explorers like Pizarro's amazing conquest of the mighty Inca empire, it was thought that El Dorado existed somewhere in the yet to be explored regions of South America. By 1595, the most likely location for El Dorado was thought to be the highlands of Guyana, marked by a terrain that was as harsh as difficult to access.

The First Journey

As soon as he received royal permission for the voyage in search of El Dorado, Raleigh began preparations in which he was supported by his half-brother Sir John Gilbert. Investors and soldiers were rallied just as ships and supplies were gathered. Eventually, on February 6, 1595, Raleigh set out on his expedition with a fleet of five small ships. The Spanish were none too happy with Raleigh's expedition since they regarded all colonial resources of South American as Spanish possessions. After their arrival at the Port of Trinidad, Raleigh sent out a team for reconnaissance so that he would have an idea about the strength of Spanish forces. Raleigh was a shrewd commander and in a swift, surprise move, the English attacked the town of San José and were able to capture it. Even better for Raleigh's purpose, they had been able to take prisoner, a high-ranking Spanish official named Antonio de Berrio who was reputed to be quite an authority on El Dorado. Having spent years on looking for this lost city of gold himself, Berrio cautioned Raleigh against giving into the obsession for El Dorado but Raleigh merely thought the Spaniard was distracting him from the search and paid no attention to the prisoner.

Leaving his ships docked at Trinidad, Raleigh set off for the search taking around a hundred men with him. He suspected that the Spanish were already planning an expedition with the same purpose and he had no intention of giving them the lead. Raleigh thought of travelling up the Orinoco River till it met the smaller Caroni River and then keeping following the latter till it led him to the lake which was widely believed to be the location of the lost city of Manoa.

Since Raleigh was in a rush to beat the rumoured Spanish expedition, he sailed up the Orinoco River with whatever kind of transport available – thus the English expedition consisted of a jumble of ship's boats, rafts and even a galley supposedly modified to sail on a river. Expectedly, the going was very slow – Raleigh's ragtag expedition was not only poorly equipped to cope with the strong currents of the powerful Orinoco River but his own crew's lack of discipline and professionalism gave him a good deal of grief.

The only ray of good fortune in the entire expedition was perhaps that Raleigh was able to befriend the indigenous tribes with his knack for charming people. Even more importantly, he used the indigenous people's hatred of the ruthless Spanish colonists to his own advantage and claimed that he was their enemy. The locals proved to be a huge help in guiding the expedition down the right course through the labyrinthine channels of the Orinoco River. Among the local people whose support proved especially beneficiary was an elderly chieftain named Topiawari. From him, Raleigh again heard of an ancient culture that lived in the mountains and had vast quantities of gold. More than ever, Raleigh was convinced that this was the fabled city of Manoa and he became desperate to find it. He sent his men to scout for gold and some of them came back with rocks which he thought would prove to be ores of the precious metal.

Meanwhile, the expedition continued to be buffeted by troubles. There were not only growing rumours about the rival Spanish expedition getting nearer but even the Orinoco River was getting increasingly difficult to navigate. The onset of heavy rains had swollen up the river and Raleigh did not relish the prospect of either being drowned by the river or ambushed by the Spanish. So even though he had not yet found the city of El Dorado or that of Manoa, he thought it more prudent to sail back to Trinidad and return to England with the hope that the rocks would be evidence enough to request from the Queen support for another expedition. And in anticipation of a future search, he struck a deal with Topiawari, promising the tribe military aid in their fight against the Spanish colonizers in exchange of local knowledge and guidance to the city of Manoa. As a sigh of his good faith in the agreement, Raleigh even left behind two of his men and decided to take Topiawari's son back with him to England.

Fortunately, the journey down the Orinoco River to the mouth was much easier as they were no longer fighting the currents. The English were relieved to find their ships still safely anchored at

Trinidad and they were all eager to return to England. On the way back, Raleigh could not help inflicting a little damage at the places in Spanish control – thus he led a successful attack on the island of Margarita and also struck at the port of Cumana where the Spanish prisoner Berrio was left off.

Finally, in August 1595, Raleigh arrived in England but did not get the kind of reception he was hoping for. News about his inability to discover El Dorado or the city of Manoa had already preceded him and he realized that his voyage was already being considered an embarrassing failure. Worse still his enemies at court had gleefully seized his failure as an opportunity to cast him out. Even the rocks he had got back failed to generate any interest in a second journey for the quest of El Dorado.

However, it was not the right time to cast off a useful soldier like Raleigh – England was gearing up for another fight against Spain and the Queen knew better than to turn away her once favourite courtier. Raleigh thus was convinced to take part in the offensive against Cadiz in 1596. However, before he could endear himself to the Queen with his services, she died in 1603 and was succeeded by James I on the throne. This was not good news for Raleigh whose enemies were finally successful in pinning him down. Raleigh was accused of treason, found guilty and imprisoned in the Tower of London where he would remain for the next twelve years.

And yet, he continued to remain an explorer at heart. Even from the prison, Raleigh was able to sponsor and organize as many as three different expeditions to Guyana in search of the fabled city of Manoa.

The Second Journey

On the strength of his past services to the crown, Raleigh was granted permission by King James I for a last trip to Guyana so that he could bring his search for El Dorado to fruition. But Raleigh had to agree not to get into any fights with the Spanish with whom James I was trying to improve relations.

However, this voyage was plagued with trouble from the very start. First of all bad weather compelled Raleigh to stop and take refuge at an Irish port after which he was attacked by the Spanish at Canary Islands as the latter mistook the English fleet for pirates. Raleigh not wanting to break his word to the king did not fight back but his rancour against the Spanish grew worse.

Again on the way to Guyana, the English expedition was beset with illness. Once they reached the Mouth of the Orinoco River, it was decided that Raleigh would remain with the ships at the port while a smaller expedition, led by his Lieutenant Laurence Keymis and his nephew George Raleigh, would explore further inland. Unfortunately, the territory was under Spanish control and this search put the English directly in the path of confrontation with the Spanish. It was not long before hostilities erupted and in the ensuing battles, the English captured the town of Santo Thome but lost many of its men, including Raleigh's own son.

Continued skirmishes with the Spanish proved exhausting and with repeated failure to come upon any place remotely resembling the city of gold, morale was sinking fast in the English camp. Raleigh took the difficult decision to return to England, though he had an inkling of what was awaiting there. True to his fears, Raleigh was arrested right after setting foot on the English shore violating his charter, according to which he was not to do anything to break the peace with Spain. Raleigh was tried, found guilty and put to death on October 29, 1618.

Raleigh's Legacy

Raleigh represented the best of the Renaissance Man – A self-made individual who not only excelled in courtly attributes of arts and culture but was also a brave warrior, determined explorer and loyal to the crown. In the context of exploration, Raleigh's achievements like discovering and naming the land of Virginia as well as founding the colony in North America may have been modest as compared to the legendary explorers like Columbus and Magellan, nevertheless, he was successful in creating a widespread interest in the science of exploration through his writings such as the *History of the World,* published in 1614.

Finally, Raleigh's most valuable achievement may have been the good relations that he established between the English and the natives of South America. His friendship with tribal chieftains such as Topiawari ensured that the English had made a precious ally against the Spanish settlers – a gift from Raleigh that would help England emerge as one of biggest colonial powers in the world.

□

13

James Cook

(1728-1779)

Though the Age of Discovery unveiled the continents of North and South American before Europe and motivated explorers to circumnavigate the globe, yet important chunks of the planet remained unexplored – most notably the southern continent of Australia with New Zealand and other Pacific lands. It would be roughly another two centuries before the world would come to know about the existence of these places through the daring journeys of a great explorer, Captain James Cook.

Early Life

Born on 27 October 1728 in a small village near Middlesbrough in Yorkshire, James Cook came from a humble background. His father was a farm hand and young James too worked on the land during his teenage years. However, at the age of 18 in a turn of events that would change his life, James was taken on as an apprentice by a Quaker ship-owner in a small seaside village near Whitby, England. This experience brought him to the coast where he was exposed to the excitement of a sailor's life and gradually the desire to try his luck at the sea began to take hold of young James.

In 1755, Cook signed up with the Royal Navy as a sailor and soon found himself heading to North America. Such was his desire to learn and prove himself an able mariner that he rapidly rose through the ranks and just at the age of 29 years he was made a ship's master. This was the Pembroke which was captured during the Seven Years War, which continued from 1756 to 1763. While in service with the Royal Navy at this time, Cook learnt to survey and chart coastal waters – something that would prove handy during his later journeys through the Pacific Ocean in the southern hemisphere. At this time in North America, though he took upon himself to map the major part of the entrance to the Saint Lawrence River. And even greater feat was mapping the uneven coastline of Newfoundland during the 1760s while he was aboard HMS Grenville. With the help of local pilots, he supervised the survey of the north-west stretch in 1763 and 1764, the south coast between the Burin Peninsula and Cape Ray in 1765 and 1766 as well as the west coast in 1767. All these achievements very soon came into the notice of the British Government and not surprisingly Cook was chosen by the government to head a scientific expedition into the southern hemisphere.

The Legend of Terra Australis

While almost the entire northern hemisphere had been charted by the explorers of Europe by the beginning of the 18th century, what lay in the southern half of the globe still remained something of a mystery. Though the Spanish had found South America, mapped and colonized it even, another land lay intriguingly just beyond reach – the mythical land of Terra Australis.

The idea of Terra Australis had existed since antiquity. Introduced by Aristotle, it was later expanded by Ptolemy, who believed that the lands of the northern hemisphere should be balanced by land in the southern hemisphere and thus there surely existed another large continent down south which enclosed the Indian Ocean. Terra Australis was thus mainly thought to be an antipodean continent, surrounding the South Pole and was seen as a land of unfulfilled promise – a kind of utopia, just waiting to be discovered and colonized by some enterprising country which would then grow rich with its unending resources.

The explorers of the Age of Discovery had discovered the southern tip of Africa and that of South America too; they had also found that the Indian Ocean could be traversed both from the western and eastern sides. Thus, the supposed location of the legendary Terra Australis receded further south, though belief in this large landmass balancing the continents of the northern hemisphere persisted.

The French Connection

The idea of Terra Australis especially struck a chord with the French in their search for new territories. Named on French maps since 1531, their ships plied back and forth across the southern ocean on voyages looking for this huge land of opportunity. And one individual who provided a major boost to these efforts was Jean Paulmier, a young priest from Normandy, who first wrote about colonising Terra Australis in 1654. Paulmier was driven by a desire to propagate Christianity in this new land and thus he vehemently urged his countrymen to set out on voyages to find a way to it. This impassioned appeal launched a succession of French voyages of discovery to an area which had till now been mainly traversed by Spanish and Portuguese explorers and a few Dutch traders. Following Paulmier's idea, 18th-century French voyagers like Bouvet de Lozier, Marion du Fresne and Yves-Joseph de Kerguelen headed south and encountered lands enveloped in ice and snow. Though these were actually part of Antarctica, at the time, they believed that behind the ice-barrier lay a temperate land of opportunity and fruition, the mythical Terra Australis.

The British Initiative

While it was the French who were mainly interested in coming upon Terra Australis, the English too were intrigued by the myth and decided to investigate the possibility of the existence of such a southern continent. The impetus came when Alexander Dalrymple, the examiner of sea journals for the English East India Company, found detailed descriptions of Terra Australis while translating some Spanish documents captured in the Philippines in 1752. He in turn published these as the, *Historical Collection of the Several Voyages and Discoveries in the South Pacific Ocean*,

Dalrymple's claim of the existence of an unknown continent aroused widespread interest and compelled the British Government to do something about it.

In 1769, a rare astronomical phenomenon had got the scientific community in Europe highly excited – the planet Venus was due to pass in front of the sun. But this event would be visible only in the southern hemisphere because of which several governments began planning on sending expeditions down south. The British Government claimed before the world that it would be a part of this unique astronomical feat and chose James Cook to head an expedition into the southern hemisphere. The expedition would also include other experts like the astronomer Charles Green and Botanist Joseph Nanks but one of its real reasons would be the search for the truth about the fabled land of Terra Australis.

The First Voyage Down South

In 1769, James Cook was chosen to command the HMS Endeavour and thus set sail for the southern hemisphere. He arrived in Tahiti in April 1769 and here the scientists on-board the Endeavour were able to observe the fantastic astronomical phenomenon of Venus passing in front of the sun. After this, the expedition moved further south and came upon the coast of New Zealand. Next, the endeavour sailed along the eastern coast of the land which later came to be known as Australia. This was a remarkable discovery since the Europeans till now had not come across this new land or even seen it from a distance. Cook claimed it for Britain and named it New South Wales. After this discovery, Cook and his crew headed back to England and arrived home in July 1771.

The Second Voyage

In 1772, with two ships, Cook set off on another voyage to the southern hemisphere – the main purpose was to find out more about the continent that he had sailed by on his previous voyage. This time he not only wished to land on the continent but explore a little inwards, if possible. However, instead of coming upon the

Australian landmass, the expedition sailed very near to the Antarctica and was forced to turn away because of the ice and bitterly cold weather. On his way back northwards, he visited New Zealand but more importantly he was able to chart numerous islands in the Pacific Ocean. These can be identified as modern-day Easter Island, Tonga, South Georgia, New Caledonia and the South Sandwich Islands. The last group of islands have an interesting story behind their name – Cook came upon these Hawaiian Islands and decided to name them the Sandwich Islands after the Earl of Sandwich, also known as John Montagu. Finally, in 1775, Cook and his second expedition returned dropped anchor on the English shore.

The Third Voyage and Death

For this third voyage of exploration, Cook chose a different destination. This time he was not interested in the fabled Terra Australis but instead a far more substantial entity – the Northwest Passage. This was a sea route thought to connect the waters of the Atlantic and Pacific Oceans through the extreme north that had been known since the time of the Vikings. Hence, in a way, the Northwest Passage was believed to provide a link between the continents of Europe and Asia through the high arctic latitudes. But cook was unable to find this rumoured route and instead turned his attention southwards. On this voyage, he explored the Hawaiian Islands and things seemed to be proceeding smoothly till a dispute emerged between the islanders and the English crew. One of the ship's boats had been stolen and in retaliation, Cook tried to take the island's chief as hostage – in the resulting skirmish, Cook was stabbed and he died on 14 February 1779.

Cook's Legacy

Cook's main contribution to the history of exploration was the charting of the Pacific, New Zealand and Australia. He provided the first accurate map of the Pacific and the results of his voyages radically changed European perceptions of world geography. Another consequence of his surveying skills was the charting of the Newfoundland Coast in North America. These were the first large-scale, scientific and accurate maps of the island's coasts and more significantly they were the first to be based on precise triangulation for determining land outlines. Their importance can be gauged by the fact that though created in late eighteenth century, the maps continued to be referred to well into the twentieth century.

Also with his second voyage to the southern seas in 1772, Cook finally put the myth of Terra Australis to rest. His voyage around most of New Zealand in 1770 proved that it was a small island in itself and could not be part of a large continent as thought by the supporters of the Terra Australis theory. On his second voyage, he circumnavigated the globe very close to the Antarctica – indeed on some occasions, his ships even crossed the south polar circle. This revealed that if there was a southern continent at all, it would have to be located well within the cold polar areas. An extension from this polar area into a land with a temperate climate, as imaged in the Terra Australis myth, thus was just not geographically possible.

Above all, James Cook was as gifted in the wealth of humanity as he was with scientific skills. His was the rare instance of an official who rose through the ranks to attain one of the highest positions in the institution when he was made the Captain of the Royal Navy. Consequently, Cook held the welfare of the ordinary sailors quite close to his heart. In keeping with this, he once introduced a diet of watercress, sauerkraut and orange extract on his ship so as to combat scurvy – a deadly disease caused by vitamin deficiency to which sailors, living on a diet of dry food on ships, were especially vulnerable.

Captain James Cook thus was a true man of the seas – explorer, navigator, cartographer and a leader of men. An idea of range of the breadth of vision can be gauged from the words that he is believed to have said after his stint in Newfoundland, that he intended to go not only, "Farther than any man has been before me, but as far as I think it is possible for a man to go" – a epitaph which can be well applied to his life in general.

□

14

David Livingstone

(1813-1873)

The inaccessibility of the interiors of Africa had always mystified European travellers. Physical barriers such the dense forests, vast deserts and mighty rivers as well as cultural ones like strange tribes had held back explorers from other parts of the world till the end of 19th century. And one of the first people to set into the heart of the African landscape was the Scottish missionary and doctor David Livingstone.

European Presence in Africa

Though most of Africa was unknown to Europeans till the 1880s, there were certain areas which had become colonized in the centuries before. Because of reasons of accessibility, most of these areas were along the coasts or short distances inland from the bigger rivers like Congo and Niger. The British for example had colonies in Sierra Leone, Gold Coast, Gambian coast as well as in Cape Colony, Natal and the Transvaal in Southern Africa while the French had a major presence in Dakar and St. Louis in Senegal, Algeria and a protectorate extending over the coastal region of Dahomey which marks modern-day Benin.

Likewise, the Portuguese had established their power as early as 1492 in Angola and later went onto extend it to Mozambique and port of Luanda. Spain controlled parts of north west Africa at Ceuta and Melilla while Turkey had traditionally influence over the Islamic regions of North Africa like Egypt, Libya, and Tunisia.

From 1880, Africa saw a sudden spurt in the arrival of European explorers and consequently in the colonizers. There were certain social, economic and political conditions originating in Europe behind this rapid colonization of Africa which is known in history as the Scramble for Africa which continued till the beginning of 20th century. A prime reason was the end to slavery and the concurrent rise of capitalism in Europe. When the slaving trade was abolished in Europe, there emerged a need for other supposedly legitimate avenues of commerce between Europe and Africa. The latter began to be seen as a continent with vast mineral and other natural resources which could serve as the source of raw materials powering the rapid industrialization of Europe. At the same time, population centres of Africa could serve as captive market for manufactured goods from Europe. Thus, all major European powers became eager to control parts of the continent and this started the Scramble for Africa.

The Role of the Explorers

The explorers also had a crucial role to play in the rush to own a piece of the African pie. The 19th century was marked by a spurt of expeditions determined to chart the interiors of the continent, especially to map the course of the Niger River and to find the city of Timbuktu, the fabled source of much wealth and treasure. To a certain extent, this was spearheaded by the African Association by wealthy Englishmen in 1788. But with the passage of the century, it became clearer that the explorers were not simply motivated by a desire for knowledge of Africa; instead they began to travel the continent in search for mineral resources, markets, natural goods as well as possible trade routes that would be of use to their wealthy patrons back in Europe.

It was this spurt of interest in Africa that provided the context for the journeys of David Livingstone. Partly influenced by a natural curiosity to 'discover', the mysterious continent and partly driven by the missionary's zeal to spread Christianity, Livingstone travelled to those parts of Africa which where a whiteman before him had never set foot.

Early Life

Born on 19 March 1813 to a working-class family in Blantyre, Scotland, David Livingstone was the second of seven children. Though at the very young age of ten, David started working for a mill company, his father ensured that the boy could read and write. Also David attended the evening school provided by the mill company. In the midst of it all, he found himself increasingly interested in natural history and even taught himself Latin to delve deeper into the subject.

In 1836 with his savings from the mill, Livingstone enrolled himself into Anderson's University, Glasgow where he studied medicine under Andrew Buchanan MD. However, after just two years, he took a break from and joined the London Missionary Society in Chipping Ongar, Essex, for a year. In 1840, he moved to London to complete his medical studies and at the end of the year he qualified as a Licentiate of the Faculty of Physicians and Surgeons of Glasgow.

Around the same time Livingstone was also ordained a missionary by the London Missionary Society and in December 1840, he left the shores of England to travel to South Africa as a missionary doctor. In March 1841, he landed in Cape Town, South Africa and from there proceeded to his further destination which was the mission station at Kuruman.

First Expedition

Livingstone's first foray into the African continent began in 1841. At this time, he was primarily interested in evangelical motives – he wanted to travel into the interiors of the continent to spread Christianity and through it supposedly 'civilize' the people. A few years into his arrival, Livingstone married a woman named Marry Moffat, with whom he had several children.

The first phase of his African exploration can be roughly grouped from the year 1842 to 1856. From his missionary location in South Africa, Livingstone decided to head north and in the process, he completed the daunting task of crossing the Kalahari Desert. In 1849, his explorations led to the shores of Lake Ngami and roughly three years later in 1851, he traced the origins of the mighty Zambezi River. Over the following two years, he travelled west and reached the Atlantic coast in the region of Luanda in 1853. Between 1853 and 1856, he travelled the breadth of Africa from west to east, starting from Luanda in Angola till he reached to Quelimane in Mozambique. During his journey in 1855, he came across one of the most famous natural sites in Africa, the Zambezi Falls which was known as the, "Smoke That Thunders", by the indigenous people. In honour of the reigning monarch of his country, Livingstone renamed the magnificent waterfall, Victoria Falls. While crossing the continent from west to east, he had become the first European in Africa to follow the course of the Zambezi River till it emptied its waters into the sea.

In 1857, Livingstone returned to England and was hailed both by the government and his countrymen for his journeys into Africa.

Second Expedition

In 1858, Livingstone was commissioned by the British Government to head an expedition that would navigate and chart the entire course of the Zambezi River. The journey proved to be a failure because of the lack of discipline and professionalism among the crew. At the same time, Livingstone's personal life too was struck with tragedy since his wife Mary died in 1862, after the couple's return to Africa. Two years later, without making much headway into the expedition, Livingstone returned to England in 1864.

Third Expedition

David Livingstone sailed from England for the last time and in early 1666 arrived on the shores of Zanzibar. The main purpose of this expedition was to trace the source of one of the most famous rivers in history, the Nile. Over the course of his travels, Livingstone came upon other water bodies but the source of the Nile eluded him. One of the most significant episodes of this journey was his halt at the hamlet of Nyangwe, where Livingstone was horrified at the sight of Arabic slave traders butchering hundreds of villagers.

Around this time, nothing was heard about Livingstone's expedition for almost four years and it was thought that the members including the explorer had got lost and probably died. In order to look for the missing people, the *London Daily Telegraph* and *New York Herald*, took a joint initiative to send an investigative team into Africa led by the charismatic journalist Henry Morton Stanley.

Encounter with Stanley

Born in Wales, Henry Morton Stanley had migrated to the United States and become a naturalized American. Though there was no dearth of courage and initiative on Stanley's part, he was primarily motivated by the prospect of lucrative contracts and fame when he agreed to set out on the search for Livingstone. Also unlike the older Scottish explorer, Stanley liked to travel in comfort and safety – it is believed that while Livingstone went about with only a few porters, Stanley had an army of bearers waiting at his every command.

On 13 November 1871, the enterprising journalist finally managed to find Livingstone at Uiji in Central Africa; as Livingstone stood on the edge of Lake Tanganyika, Stanley is believed to have approached him with the words which have gone down in history as an icon of understatement, "Dr. Livingstone, I presume?"

Livingstone supposed reply, "You have brought me new life", was equally significant since the missionary doctor had missed on many of the defining moments in the history of the world like Franco-Prussian War, the opening of the Suez Canal as well as the inauguration of the transatlantic telegraph.

Among all the people who led exploration expeditions in Africa, Stanley is the one most closely connected to the start of the Scramble for Africa through the treaties that he fixed between King Leopold II of Belgium and the African tribal chiefs along the River Congo. The idea was to create a region of influence for Belgium and this instigated other European countries to do the same through other explorers like the German Carl Peters.

His Death

During his final years Livingstone was beset with health problems, but he refused to leave Africa. Despite Stanley's offer to take him back to Europe, Livingstone chose to stay and go on with his mission to find the source of the Nile. Eventually, he contracted dysentery and in May 1873, died in the swamps around Lake Bangweulu. After his death his body was returned to Britain for burial in Westminster Abbey.

His Legacy

Today Livingstone is chiefly remembered for his journeys through regions in Africa where no European had ever set foot, especially in the southern and central parts of the continents. He was the first European to cross the width of southern Africa.

At the same time though, his legacy as a doctor and missionary is highly significant. Not only was he one of the first medical missionaries to enter southern Africa but actually the first to venture into central Africa. More importantly, he was often the first European to reach out to chieftains of the local tribes. Because of his humane and compassionate nature, he did not have difficulty in winning the trust of the people – this was made only easier by the wealth of his medical knowledge. In fact, he was so highly sought out by the native population for his healing skills that over time he had to restrict his treatment to the most serious patients.

Yet another medical field where Livingstone's contribution proved extremely valuable was the discovery of the cause of and treatment of malaria. More than 30 years before Ronald Ross established the link between mosquitoes and malaria, Livingstone had already suggested that the two were related. More importantly, Livingstone was one of the first to determine the appropriate dosage of quinine that would be effective against malaria. As proof of his success, the rate of death from malaria among his crew members was far lower than in other expeditions. Known as, 'Livingstone's Rousers', a formula of his anti-malarial quinine drug appeared in his travel writings and subsequently manufactured by the pharmaceutical company Burroughs Wellcome which was in circulation till as late as the 1920s.

Livingstone later also found a relation between the bite of the tampan (tick) as well as relapsing fever. Most importantly for later medical knowledge, over the course of his travels through Africa, Livingstone was able to draw causal links between environmental factors and diseases such as pneumonia, typhoid and dysentery.

Finally, a crucial part of Livingstone's legacy is made up of his writings. He was not only a prolific writer but a close and accurate observer as well. The journals, letters and travelogues that he has left behind are a goldmine of first-hand observations on the landscape, the cultures and the sheer variety of Africa. One of his most important works is, *Narrative of an expedition to the Zambesi and its tributaries; and of the discovery of the Lakes Shirwa and Nyassa (1858-1864) which reveals his strong stand* against slavery. Another work, *Missionary Travels and Researches in South Africa*, was published in 1857.

Though in the beginning of his years in Africa, Livingstone's missionary zeal fuelled much of his exploration often ignoring the indigenous faiths, towards the end he was fascinated by the natural and cultural wealth of the land and kept going on. And finally though his belief in the commercial prospects of Africa has been pointed out by some critics as paving the way for colonialism, knowing Livingstone's innate faith in the dignity of Africans, it is likely that he himself would have opposed the imperialistic agenda of the European powers.

□

15

Sacagawea

(C. 1788-1812)

The history of world exploration has been primarily written by male figures – famous navigators, travellers and scientists have been overwhelmingly men, at least till the modern age. The most natural reason for this is that women, because of their maternal responsibilities and the lack of safety, found it prudent to stay within the familiar geographical context. Even then there have been some female figures in history – and increasingly more in the modern age – who took on the challenge of setting out for new places and succeeded too. One of the earliest of women explorers is Sacagawea, of the Lehmi Shoshone Indian tribe who acted as a guide and translator in the 1804-06 Lewis-Clarke expedition of America and played a crucial role in the discovery of a route to the hitherto unexplored North-western part of the country.

Early Life

Details from the early part of Sacagawea's life are very sketchy. She was believed to have been born around 1788 in the Lehmi River Valley in present-day Idaho of the US. In around 1800, when she must have been roughly twelve years of age, she was kidnapped by Hidatsa Indians, also known as the Minitari tribe and taken from native place to what constitutes modern-day North Dakota. The following year, she along with another girl was sold by the Hidatsa men to a French-Canadian fur trader and explorer named Toussaint Charbonneau and became his wives.

According to some reports, Charbonneau either purchased Sacagawea from the Hidatsa people or won her while gambling. In 1805, Sacagawea bore a son to Charbonneau who was named, Jean-Baptiste Charbonneau, also lovingly known as Little Pomp.

The Clark-Lewis Expedition

In 1803, President Thomas Jefferson of United States made an appeal before the Congress for funding of an expedition to be led by two explorers Meriwether Lewis and William Clarke. These two intended to travel through the western territories that started from the Missouri River and continued till the land emptied out into the Pacıfic Ocean.

The idea of such an expedition had been fermenting for some time in President Jefferson's mind. As early as 1792, he was interested in sending a team cross the North American continent, almost a decade before he became President. He had even sent a proposal to the Philadelphia-based American Philosophical Society to finance an expedition to explore the west, but the plan did not take off. In the summer of 1802, Jefferson happened to read a book by Alexander Mackenzie, a Scottish explorer who had travelled across Canada to the Pacific Ocean and back. The President shared the parts of the book with his personal secretary Meriwether Lewis and gradually the seed of the idea of north-westward exploration took root.

Though Jefferson was largely motivated by a sense of adventure for setting such an expedition into motion, he also knew that in order to obtain funding from the Congress, a far more practical reason needed to be highlighted. At the time trapping of wild animals in the northwest was a highly profitable activity and the British had a strong hold in this trade, in this part of the continent. Jefferson based his appeal for funding on grounds that if this expedition were to take off, the US could benefit from building hospitable relations with the Native Indian tribes in the northwest and in the process establish a foothold in the lucrative fur trade. In fact, a portion of the funds allocated to the expedition would be set aside for buying gifts for Native Indian Chieftains; such items usually ranged from medals for their symbolic value to cooking implements which had a more practical use.

One of the main principles of the proposed expedition was that it was not to be designed as an attempt to claim territory in the northwest or establishing dominance over the indigenous people living there. Instead the aim was to establish friendly relations which could eventually help with American trade interests. For all these purposes, President Jefferson made an appeal of appropriation $2,500 from the Congress. Though initially some doubts were raised in Congress about the likelihood of the achievement of the expedition's aims, eventually the funding came through.

Though the establishment of settlements in the remote northwest was never the primary aim of the expedition, the increasing presence of people from other countries like Britain and Russia in the Pacific Northwest was fast becoming a concern for President Jefferson. He and other guardians of the country were worried that just like the Atlantic Coast had been settled by people from various European countries like the Dutch, French, Irish and Spanish apart from the British, the same kind of settlement would appear on the western coast. Hence, one of the covert aims of the Clark-Lewis expedition was probably the survey of the northwest to examine the possibilities of future full-fledged travel or even maybe settlement. In fact, according to some historians, United States' claim to the Oregon Territory can be actually traced back to the success of the Lewis and Clark Expedition.

However, more important was the desire to find out more about what lay in the north-western heart of the country. During the expedition, Clark and Lewis painstakingly recorded all their experiences in journals and drew maps of the routes, all of which went a long way in adding to people's understanding about the north-western part of the continent.

Preparations for the Expedition

Even before the expedition took final shape, President Jefferson saw to it that Meriwether Lewis received a thorough grounding in science. The young man was sent to Philadelphia to receive training from eminent scientists such as Dr. Benjamin Rush and reputed surveyors such as Andrew Ellicott who showed Lewis how to use equipments like the sextant and octant to navigate through uncharted territories, map their geographical locations and even take measurements of natural features.

Apart from this, Lewis was also instructed in the flora and fauna of that part of the country as well as the ways of identifying any new species of plants and animals that the expedition might encounter. All such training would prove invaluable to the documentation as well as increased understanding of the north-western part of the country.

An important part of the preparations was the choice of William Clark as one of the leaders of the expedition. Having served in the United States Army, Clark would safeguard the team if faced by Native American hostilities. Though the mandate of the expedition was to avoid military action, nevertheless a veteran like Clark was thought to inspire confidence within the travellers regarding their safety.

Another matter to be decided was the correct size of the expedition – too small a group would be vulnerable to potentially inimical tribes while too large a group would put indigenous people on their guard and banish any chances of peaceful collaboration. For this, a select group of volunteers was chosen from the United States Army who would be known as the Corp of Discovery and go onto make up the most vital part of the Clark-Lewis expedition.

In 1804, Meriwether and Clark began active preparations for their trek through the northwest. In the Corps of Discovery, arrived at the Hidatsa-Mandan villages and the Fort Mandan was built on the Missouri River. After this, the explorers started looking for Native American Indians who could act as guides and translators through their journey from the Missouri River to the Pacific Ocean.

Sacagawea Joins the Expedition

Eight volumes of journals painstakingly written by Lewis and Clark, today give an idea about Sacagawea's role in the expedition. The travellers knew that they would require horses to cross the Bitterroot Mountains and among the local tribes, the Shoshones possessed horses. The captains of the expedition surmised that having someone from the tribe could give the team an edge when trading for horses on their way to the western mountains. Thus,

Sacagawea was hired along with her husband Charbonneau to work as an interpreter team for the expedition. Though Sacagawea did not speak English, she spoke Shoshone and Hidatsa. Her husband on the other hand spoke Hidatsa and French. Thus, whatever needed to be communicated from the Shoshone people to the English-speaking expedition was first passed through Sacagawea who translated the Shoshone to Hidatsa and then to Charbonneau who translated the Hidatsa to French. Thereupon the Corps' Francois Labiche took over as he spoke French and English. In this way, the words of the Shoshone people would be eventually translated into English for the captains of the team.

When the preparations for the trek began in full swing, Sacagawea was pregnant with her first child. By the time the Clark-Lewis expedition set off, Sacagawea had given birth to a baby boy who would be named Jean Baptiste and would also make the entire trip and back, snugly resting in a sling on his mother's body.

As the only woman in a 33 member expedition, Sacagawea's contribution to its success was manifold. Apart from her translating for the expedition and thus ensuring the captains could negotiate with the Indian tribes in the right manner, her traditional survival skills were of great help to the well-being of the expedition. She was extremely knowledgeable about where edible roots, plants and berries could be found in the forests – all of these were used as food and sometimes, even as medicine. Apart from these, she cooked, sewed, mended and cleaned the clothes of the men of the team.

In one incident, Sacagawea's courage and presence of mind proved valuable for the expedition. On May 14, 1805, rough weather hit the boat, Sacagawea was riding in and it almost capsized. However, she was able to save many important papers and supplies that would otherwise have been lost. Indeed her calm strength in a situation of great danger impressed the captains of the team and the rest of the men.

On August 12, 1805, a scout group sent by Captain Lewis across the Continental Divide at modern-day Lemhi Pass was met by a band of Shoshone people. Incredibly enough, the leader of the Shoshones turned out to be Sacagawea's own brother with whom she had lost touch after being kidnapped as a twelve-year old by the Hidatsa people. Meeting after five years of separation, Sacagawea had an emotional reunion with her brother who in turn was able to help the expedition with horses and other supplies.

On many occasions, Sacagawea with her mere presence was able to save the expedition from potential trouble. As the team travelled westward, it encountered many strange tribes who had never seen whitemen before. Any possibility of conflict was greatly reduced when the Indians noticed a woman in the midst of the expedition and that too with an infant. In this way, Sacagawea's presence earned the team valuable trust and goodwill which were crucial for their passage through the unexplored northwest.

Finally, on November 24, 1805, the expedition arrived at their destination – the point where the Columbia River emptied into the Pacific Ocean. Here a vote was taken from all the members of the expedition on whether to settle down for the winter – and Sacagawea's vote was counted along with those of the captains and other men. This showed the extent of regard she enjoyed within the team and how much her opinion was valued by others. On the basis of the results of the election, the expedition decided to stay back on the Pacific Coast. For the purpose, in Fort Clatsop was built at a site near modern-day Astoria, Oregon, in which the team waited out the winter of 1805-06.

Her Last Years

After the winter passed, the Clark-Lewis expedition started their return journey. As the team once again passed through the Shoshone settlements, Sacagawea's childhood tracking skills proved valuable. She guided the expedition through trails and routes that they could not have found on their own. One of the most important discoveries made with Sacagawea's help was what is now is known as Bozeman Pass, Montana which was then described as "a large road passing through a gap in the mountain," and which led the team to the Yellowstone River.

At long last on August 14, 1806, the Clark-Lewis expedition was back in the Hidatsa-Mandan villages which had marked their starting point almost two years ago. This was also where the interpreter team of Sacagawea and her husband Charbonneau together with their boy left the team. In keeping with the conventions of the time, Sacagawea was not paid anything while her husband was given $500.33 and 320 acres of land as payment for services rendered to the Clark-Lewis expedition.

A few years after the end of the expedition, Clark is believed to have arranged for Sacagawea and Charbonneau to settle in St. Louis. Around that time, Sacagawea gave birth to a girl who was named Lisette. On December 22, 1812, aged only 24, Sacagawea died from unknown causes. After her death, Clark legally adopted her two children. While the fate of the daughter, Lisette was lost to obscurity, there is record of Jean Baptiste growing up and receiving education in St. Louis and Europe. Eventually, he became a linguist and later returned to his native mountains of northwest America.

Sacagawea's Legacy

Very few mentions of women exist in mainstream history of exploration of the world. Though now feminist scholars are digging through mounds of research material to come up with names like fanny bullock workman, Mary Henrietta Kingsley and Janet Wulsin who broke social conventions to set out on adventurous journeys and voyages, still they are not very recognizable by the masses. In contrast, Sacagawea's legacy has enjoyed widespread popularity, especially in the United States. According to some, she has the most number of statues erected in her honour than any other woman in the US. A large number of public institutions as well as natural features like are mountain peaks, streams and lakes in the northwest bear the name of Sacagawea.

In July 1998, the then US Treasury Secretary Rubin announced that an image of Sacagawea would be chosen as the face of the new dollar coin. Though the decision led to some controversy since it ended up replacing the Susan B. Anthony coin, eventually the choice of Sacagawea put the seal on her rightful place in the annals of the great explorers of the world.

□

16

John Lloyd Stephens

(1805-1852)

Though Central and South America had been discovered by European explorers during the Age of Discovery, large parts of the continents still held within its dense forests mysteries of grand civilizations from ancient times. One such magnificent ancient civilization was that of the Mayas which was revealed to the modern world by famous explorer and archaeologist, John Lloyd Stephens. Together with his travelling companion Frederick Catherwood, Stephens became famous for his exploration of ancient Maya ruins. To a large extent, the popularity of the duo was due to their best-selling book, *Incidents of Travel in Central America, Chiapas and Yucatán*, first published in 1841 which detailed their journeys through Mexico, Guatemala and Honduras, looking for Maya sites and revealing their grandeur and beauty to the larger world.

Early Life

Born in 1805, at the Shrewsbury township of New Jersey, John Lloyd Stephens was the second son of a successful New Jersey merchant, Benjamin Stephens. Soon the family moved to New York City and there young Stephens grew up to the best of educational opportunities. Stephens was taught about the Classics at two privately tutored schools and when only thirteen, he enrolled at the Columbia University. Four years later, he graduated at the top of his class.

Next Stephens worked as a student-at-law for a year after which he signed up at the Law School at Litchfield in Connecticut. After getting his law degree, Stephens came back to New York City and started practicing law.

After around eight years as a legal practitioner in New York, Stephens decided to take a break and embark on a long journey. In keeping with his love of the Classics and ancient civilizations, he decided to head for Europe and particularly explore the archaeological ruins around the Mediterranean region. During this time, he visited countries as diverse as France, Italy, Greece, Turkey as well as Russia, Poland and later Egypt too. So widespread were his travels, that very soon he began to be known as the, "American Traveller". After his return, he also penned a book about his journeys through the different places in the Levant.

Meeting with Catherwood

During the course of his travels in Europe, Stephens arrived in London in 1836. Here he met Frederick Catherwood, an English artist and architect and the two discovered a common love of adventure. Before meeting Stephens, Catherwood had travelled extensively through the ancient archaeological sites in Mediterranean. He visited countries like Turkey, Greece, Egypt and Palestine between the years 1824 and 1832 and devoted himself to drawing the monuments made by the ancient Egyptians, Carthaginians and Phoenicians. In 1833, Catherwood spent around six weeks in Jerusalem and was probably the only European at the time to have made a thorough survey of the famous Dome of the Rock there. The result of all these works was that Catherwood came to be widely known as a topographical artist and especially became famous for his use of a specific drawing technique with the aid of *camera lucida,* an instrument that reproduced the image of the object on a sheet of paper so that an outline could then be traced.

Catherwood's meeting with Stephens in London in 1836 changed the course of the lives of both men. After realizing they shared a fascination for ancient archaeological remains, both developed an interest in the ruins of ancient Maya civilizations in Central America. This was the result of their coming across a book by a 19th-century Central American explorer and army officer named Juan Galindo whose description of the ruins was the first to note the similarity between the contemporary Maya peoples and the carved images of the ancient Maya to be found amongst the ruins.

Both Stephens and Catherwood were extremely influenced by Galindo's book and it was not long before Catherwood agreed to Stephens' plans of touring the interiors of Central America with the intention of exploring the ancient Maya ruins.

Preparations for the Journey

Though Stephens was fired with enthusiasm about exploring the ruins of ancient Maya civilization, he was not the man to set out on a wild goose chase. His early grounding in the Classics as well as his legal training had ensured that he had a disciplined way of going about his plans. Accordingly, he made a careful survey of all the available resources on the ruins of old Mesoamerican civilization; there were not many that seemed authentic. One valuable source was made up of the descriptions of the flora, fauna and topography of Central and South America complied by the highly respected geographer, Alexander von Humbolt. Another was a book by Juan Galindo's, a Spanish officer of Central America who had documented the architectural details in the Maya ruins of the ancient cities of Copan and Palenque. Another useful guide seemed a report on ancient Maya remains compiled by one Captain Antonio del Rio which had been published in London in 1822 and accompanied with illustrations by Frederick Waldeck.

Stephens' preparations for the journey into the land of Maya ruins received an unexpected thrust when in 1839 US President, Martin Van Buren, appointed him as Special Ambassador to Central America. At the same time, there was also a churn in regional politics and the government of the Federal Republic of Central America entered into a state of civil war. In keeping with his responsibilities as a diplomat, Stephens arrived at British Honduras, now known as Belize, in the October of 1839. He was accompanied by Frederick Catherwood and for the next year, Stephens would try and alternate his political duties with travels to the sites of ancient Maya ruins.

Exploration at Copan

After landing in British Honduras in October 1839, Stephens and Catherwood proceeded to the ancient city of Copan. Located in the extreme southeast of the Mesoamerican cultural region, historians now believe that Copan was probably the capital city of a major Classic period kingdom from the 5th to 9th centuries AD. When Stephens and Catherwood came upon the magnificent remains of this ancient city, they could hardly believe that it had been constructed by the ancestors of the modern Maya people. Awed by the grandeur and lavish scale of the architecture, Stephens and Catherwood remained in Copan for few weeks with the purpose of mapping the site and making drawings.

According to a popular myth, Stephens was supposed to have purchased the rights to the ruins of Copan for the paltry sum of fifty dollars so that he could transfer the remains to the museums of United States. This has been proved to be an exaggeration and what probably happened in reality was that Stephens purchased the right to draw and chart the old buildings and sculptures at the site of Copan.

At Copan while Stephens supervised the mapping of the ruins and painstakingly jotted down his observations on the architecture and sculptures of the site, Catherwood made detailed drawings of the landscape. Especially, impressive were his etchings of the site core and the carved stones that this Maya location eventually became famous for.

Exploration at Palenque

After they had spent several weeks at Copan, Stephens and Catherwood then decided to head to Palenque, a city state from the ancient Maya civilization located in around southern Mexico that flourished in the 7th century. Though not as large as Copan,

Palenque was discovered to contain some of the finest sculptures and architectural features like the roof comb and bas-relief carvings wrought by the hands of the ancient Mayas.

In order to arrive at Palenque, Stephens and Catherwood started for Mexico from the site of Copan. However, on the way, they found themselves in Guatemala and hence decided to explore another ancient Maya site, Quiriguá. Again as they were winding their way to Palenque, they decided to pass by Tonina in the Chiapas highlands. The structures at this site date from the 6th century through the 9th centuries AD, during the Classic period. Among the highlights at this site were groups of temple pyramids set up on a terrace as well as comparatively well-preserved stucco work.

It was not before April 1840 that the explorers were able to reach Palenque. Here, they set up base at the palace and stayed for almost a month. Stephens documented various fantastic remains like the Temple of the Cross, the Temple of the Inscriptions, Temple of the Foliated Cross and the magnificent the Temple of the Sun. Likewise, Catherwood made exquisite drawings of the architectural and sculptural splendours of this ancient civilization and his Portrayal of the Temple of the Inscriptions as well as the Cross Group are considered among the most accurate drawings of the time. At Palenque, the explorers stayed for more than two months of studying, surveying and mapping the ruins but after Catherwood contracted malaria, they left in early June.

Explorations at Uxmal

After leaving Palenque, the duo headed to the Yucatan Peninsula where Stephens intended to visit Hacienda Uxmal, a huge farm owned by Simon Peon. This individual was one of the richest landowners of Mexico and had extensive property all over the Yucatan Peninsula. Peon had been introduced to Stephens in New York and the latter had expressed an interest in visiting the area to look for ancient Maya ruins.

Upon reaching Uxmal, Stephens set off right away to explore the archaeological remains of the Maya City and as Catherwood was still too weak from his illness, the artist could not go along. However, the next day the Catherwood insisted on accompanying Stephens and the duo were able to document the beauties of the site, both in words and images. Among the highlights of the site were the House of the Governor, the House of the Nuns – now referred to as the Nunnery Quadrangle – as well as the House of the Dwarf, also known as the Pyramid of the Magician. Though Stephens' notes on this site included precious information about the ruins, Catherwood's drawings were particularly appreciated for their rendering of the delicate Puuc architecture as well as the beauty of other site buildings.

Despite the wealth of archaeological remains at Uxmal, Stephens and Catherwood were compelled to leave soon as the artist continued to suffer from ill-health. They landed in New York on July 31, 1840 which means that they had been gone for almost ten months.

Second Journey to Yucatan

Though the explorers had been compelled to return early from Uxmal, the thought of archaeological treasures at Yucatan waiting to be discovered made Stephens want to return back to Central America. In 1841, thus Stephens and Catherwood made a second journey to Yucatan which continued till next year.

Later Years

Upon returning from his second trip to Yucatan, Stephens entered the steamship business and incorporated the Ocean Steam Navigation Company. Eventually, in 1849, he was made the vice-president of the newly-found Panama Railroad Company and was given the responsibility of laying of the railroad in the Central American country. He spent almost three years personally supervising the work but in 1852 he fell seriously ill with malaria and died. Three years later Stephens' former colleague and artist, Catherwood died when the steamship he was riding in sank in 1855.

The Legacy of Stephens

Together with his friend and fellow explorer Catherwood, Stephens can be credited for bringing the splendours of ancient Maya civilization before the world. Upon their return from the first journey into Central America, they published, *Incidents of Travel in Central America, Chiapas and Yucatán*, first published in 1841 which went onto became a best-seller. The book not only contain lively descriptions by Stephens of several ancient Maya sites, but the exquisite illustrations by Catherwood brought the ancient ruins almost to life. Till then only a small amount of information on ancient Mesoamerica existed and, *Incidents of Travel* not only turned out to be far superior in the accuracy of depiction as well as breadth of the coverage but caught the public imagination on the subject of Maya ruins like never before.

After Stephens and Catherwood returned from their second trip to Yucatan, they published, *Incidents of Travel in Yucatan*, in 1843 according to which the explorers had till now visited more than a total of forty Maya sites. The next year Catherwood published, *Views of Ancient Monuments in Central America, Chiapas and Yucatan*, with 25 colour lithographs he had made at various ruins.

Modern historians point out that despite all his goodwill and erudition Stephens still thought in terms of a colonial in the sense that he wanted to buy the Maya ruins for the purpose of displaying them in American museums. Also, for all his expertise in documentation, Stephens was unable to accept that the ancestors of the native Mayans could have built these cities and instead put forward the hypothesis that they must have been built by some ancient population which had now disappeared. However, for all the limitation in his thinking, Stephens together with his illustrator Catherwood was the first to dismiss the notion that these ancient cities were built by the Egyptians or some mythical race like that of Atlantis or the lost Tribe of Israel; this eventually proved to be crucial for the re-discovery of the past glory of the ancient Maya civilization.

□

17

Roald Amundsen

(1872-C.1928)

By the beginning of the 20th century, the human race had made its mark on almost every habitable part of the globe. No continent that could be settled was now left for the explorers to stamp with their flag – no continent except perhaps the icy and freezing polar regions. The race to be the first to reach the Arctic and Antarctic Circle makes one of the most thrilling adventure stories of modern times and one man who will forever loom large in the history of polar exploration is that of Norwegian Roald Amundsen who on December 14, 1911 became the first human being to reach the South Pole.

The Beginning of Polar Exploration

The history of human attempt to reach the Poles began with the exploration of the Arctic Circle since this was the most accessible and the one that humans knew something about as opposed to the Antarctic region which till Captain Cooks voyage, largely a mystery. The very first expeditions to the coldest lands of the North took place around 16th century and were primarily in search for the elusive but famous Northwest Passage – a fabled sea route supposed to exist somewhere north of the North American continent which would connect the Atlantic and Pacific Oceans. The main purpose of the search for the Northwest Passage was to seek a trade route from Europe to the Orient, that was shorter than the land route across the Mediterranean and Central Asia.

Interestingly, around the same time that explorers were looking for the fabled Northwest Passage, some were keen on charting a Northeast Passage, which would take ships around Eurasia. Though these expeditions did not succeed in discovering a realistic alternate route to the Orient, they were able to find out about the lands and smaller islands near the Arctic Circle.

One of the biggest crews to be lost in the search of Northwest Passage belonged to Sir John Franklin who left England in 1845 with two Royal Navy ships and never returned. After this the attention of the explorers turned from the Northwest Passage to the North Pole and during the last decades of the nineteenth century, there was a series of expeditions that claimed to have reached "furthest north". Finally, Robert Peary, along with Matthew Henson and Inuit explorers Oatah, Egingwah, Seegloo, and Ookeah took a dog sledge from Cape Columbia on Ellesmere Island and arrived at the North Pole on April 6, 1909.

In the Southern Hemisphere, there existed a legend of a land of bounty and temperate climate known as Terra Australis. This was thought to be located at some point beyond the barrier of ice and snow which had first been encountered by some explorers as they sailed far south along the eastern coast of the South American continent. Magellan was the first to pass from the Atlantic to the Pacific Ocean around the southern tip of the continent of South America.

Later on other explorers would explore the Pacific Ocean still further. In 1772, with two ships, Cook set off on his second voyage to the southern hemisphere. Though the main purpose was to find out more about the continent that would later come to be known as Australia, he actually ended by sailing very near to the icy landmass of Antarctica and in fact at some even passed through the South Polar Circle. However, he could not land there because of the ice and bitterly cold weather and turned away to sail through other islands of the Pacific Ocean. The significance of this voyage was that it finally did away with the myth of Terra Australis and revealed that if there was a southern continent at all, it would have to be located well within the cold polar areas.

The North Pole was usually the first choice of explorers looking to crack the Polar race; so when in 1909 Robert Peary and his team became the first people to arrive at the North Pole, other explorers in the fray turned their attention to the South Pole. Captain Robert Falcon Scott was one of the earliest explorers to have set foot on Antarctica as part of the Discovery Expedition, funded by the British Government. Scott's young colleague on Discovery, Ernest Shackleton managed to convince a private sponsor to fund his own voyage to the South Pole and even managed to reach within 160 km of the Pole but could not go the whole way because of weather hazards. When Scott learnt that Shackleton's attempt on the Pole had been unsuccessful, the Captain was determined to reach it himself and set out preparing for the expedition amidst much media attention. Little did he know, that at the same time, a young Norwegian was planning to beat him to the race to the South Pole.

Early Life of Roald Amundsen

Born into a family of Norwegian merchant sea captains in 1872, Roald Engebreth Gravning Amundsen grew up listening to stories of the cold polar regions bound in ice and snow. As he grew older, he began preparing himself to set off on polar voyages; he apparently slept with all windows open during bitterly cold Norwegian winters so as to get his body conditioned to freezing polar temperatures.

As a young man, Amundsen was fascinated by the Antarctica since the time he first glimpsed its frozen terrain in 1897. This happened when Amundsen joined the Belgian Antarctic Expedition led by Adrien de Gerlache. The ship on which they set sail was named, Belgica and Amundsen was the first mate. This expedition eventually became significant as the first to travel to in Antarctica during winter.

Crossing the Northwest Passage

Before he made an attempt to reach there on his own, he decided to garner some valuable experience in sailing to polar regions. Thus, in 1903, Amundsen set off on a voyage to traverse the Northwest Passage. At the helm of a seventy-feet fishing vessel, he had to take navigate through an ice-bound sea route that was weaved dangerously between the northern Canadian mainland and Canada's Arctic Islands. The route that Amundsen took was through Baffin Bay, Parry Channel and then southwards passing Peel Sound, James Ross Strait, Simpson Strait and Rae Strait. The crew was forced to spend two winters at King William Island which is known now as Gjoa Haven in the Nunavut region of Canada. During this time, Amundsen picked up polar survival skills from the indigenous people near Arctic lands – like using sled dogs to carry supplies and the superiority of animal skins in warding off cold and snow as opposed to heavy, woollen parkas, which if wet, would worsen the cold. All these lessons would turn out to be extremely valuable in his future expedition to the South Pole.

It took Amundsen a long agonizing three years to complete the voyage as the ship would often get stuck in the ice sheets of the Arctic Circle. When finally he arrived at Norway, he received the news that a native of Great Britain Ernst Shackleton had been the one to reach furthest south in Antarctica but came back after going up to less a hundred miles from the South Pole.

Preparations for Journey to South Pole

In April 1909, Robert Peary and his crew became the first to reach the North Pole and hence Amundsen turned his attention to the South Pole. But no one came to know of his real destination and for a long time it was thought that he was preparing for a journey to the North Pole. Amundsen had been careful to keep his intention hidden from Norwegian government officials too. This was because Amundsen knew about the weight of British influence on world affairs and feared that if word got out of his plan to reach South Pole, his government would be pressurized by Britain to call off the journey. It was only when Amundsen's ship Fram had cleared the shores of Morocco that he revealed to his crew the real destination of the expedition – the South Pole.

Though Amundsen had kept the real destination under wraps, he had ensured that preparations for the expedition were thorough.

Amundsen was widely regarded for his organization skills as for his courage as an explorer. He was determined to take every precaution against failure and foolproof the expedition against eventualities as much as humanly possible. He pored over every detail of Shackleton's journey and tried to glean any lessons from it that he could. When selecting his crew, he was particular about choosing only those personalities which would do work well as a team and was suited to long harsh weather conditions as existed in the polar regions.

One of the most crucial parts of Amundsen's preparations to the South Pole was the decision to use sled dogs. For this purpose, specially bred and trained sled dogs were selected to be part of the expedition. They had were the result of centuries of natural selection and hence were not only capable of weathering the extreme cold of Antarctica but were extremely intelligent creatures. No wonder, then a man as taciturn as Amundsen is said to have referred to them as, "our children" and even admit that, "The dogs are the most important thing for us. The whole outcome of the expedition depends on them." In fact, it is possible Amundsen's decision to use sled dogs ultimately ensured their success especially when considered against Scott's decision to use Siberian ponies and his eventual failure. Though Scott was singularly unlucky in getting the worst of polar weather, it is quite possible that Amundsen's sled dogs gave him an edge in speed and flexibility.

Reaching the South Pole

After several months of preparation and the long voyage from Europe to Antarctica, Amundsen's team made their final push for South Pole on October 18, 1911. The expedition took off from the Bay of Whales, on Antarctica's Ross Ice Shelf and was lucky to be aided by good weather. Finally at around 3 pm on December 14, 1911, Roald Amundsen became the first human to reach the South Pole where he raised the flag of Norway and named the spot Polheim or "Pole Home." On January 25, 1912, Amundsen and his team returned to their base camp, after crossing some 1,860 miles and 99 days since their departure.

The significance of Amundsen's feat in being the first to reach the South Pole becomes even more apparent when contrasted to the vagaries of fate suffered by Robert Scott. The British explorer had set out around the same time as Amundsen on the journey to reach the South Pole. But luck was not in his favour – severe blizzards and near zero visibility forced Scott and his team to stay inside the tents while Amundsen's team made precious headway on another route. Because of the long delay, Scott not only lost out the chance to reach the Pole first but rations of his team were severely depleted by the time they started for their return journey. At the same time, the approaching autumn in the Antarctica brought on terrible weather and on March 29, 1912, Scott made the final entry into his log book. The frozen bodies of the explorers were found eight months later – the site of their death was only eleven miles from a station stocked with food and supplies.

Other Polar Expeditions

In 1918, Amundsen set off to find a way through the Northeast Passage – a sea route that was believed to connect Atlantic Ocean to the Pacific Ocean from the West to East direction. Eventually, this route came to be known as the Northern Sea Route and was determined along the Russian Arctic coast from Murmansk on the Barents Sea, passing Siberia, then reaching the Bering Strait and finally the Far East.

When Amundsen began the voyage in 1918 on his ship Maud, he intended to sail along the Siberian coast and travel further than anyone had to the north and east – in the process he hoped to explore hitherto unknown areas of the Arctic Ocean. However, the ship got stuck within the ice sheets many times in the seas and had to spend three bitterly cold winters there. It would be in 1921 before Maud, would be able to break free from the ice and sail south to arrive at Seattle.

In June 1922, Amundsen decided to divide his expedition into two parts – one an aerial journey in which he would attempt to fly over the North Pole and the other would be a nautical one in which Maud, under command of Wisting would resume the original plan of drifting over the North Pole in the ice. However, both plans came to nought and led Amundsen into heavily into debt.

Amundsen though did not give up his dream of flying over the North Pole and in 1926 he along with a team of fifteen men became the first to fly over the Arctic Circle in an airplane named Norge.

His Death

Considering Amundsen's lifelong fascination with the polar regions, it hardly seems surprising that this is where he would meet his death too. In 1928, while flying on a rescue mission, Amundsen's plane crashed into the Arctic Ocean and he died. Not long before in an interview to a journalist, he had talked about his beloved Arctic region, "If only you knew how splendid it is up there, that's where I want to die."

His Legacy

A powerfully built man over six feet tall, Amundsen was proud of being popularly referred to as the, "last of the Vikings". An impeccable organizer and a daring explorer, he was a man of few words but high principles. His crew members respected him for his firm by fair way of dealing and he was affectionately referred to as "the chief."

Amundsen's chief claim to fame lies in leading the first successful expedition to the South Pole. And although his nautical expeditions over the North Pole were not successful, they were able to add to the store of available scientific knowledge about the Arctic region. The scientist Sverdrup – whom Amundsen had taken along the journey had painstakingly made records of the expedition which later were proven to be of considerable value. Finally, in 1926, Amundsen also became part of the first aerial expedition over the North Pole, thus in effect becoming one of two men – the other being fellow Norwegian and his team member Oscar Wisting – to be the first to reach each geographical pole, by ground or by air.

□

18

Sir Edmund Hillary

(1919-2008)

Sir Edmund Hillary is best known as the first whiteman to have reached the summit of the highest mountain peak on earth – the mighty Mount Everest looming above all else on the planet at 8849 metres. He shared this achievement with Tibetan co-climber Tenzing Norgay on May 29, 1953. Hillary followed his stunning feat by other journeys of adventure like leading the ascent to Mount Herschel and more significantly participating in expeditions to the South Pole. In the later part of his life, he became involved in philanthropic work and tirelessly worked for the Sherpa community in Nepal without whose help he admitted, he might not have won the race for Mount Everest.

The Challenge of Mount Everest

By the beginning of the 20th century, European and American explorers had reached all continents of the earth and made them part of the body of geographical and political world knowledge. Though most lands like the Americas, Africa, Australia and New Zealand had been marked by human presence for years before the European explorers landed on their shores, with their 'discovery' followed large-scale human settlement and modern scientific exploration. The Arctic and Antarctic were the last continents to be charted by man and when in 1909 Peary reached the North Pole – though amidst competing claims by Frederick Cook – and in 1911 Amundsen touched the South Pole, human dominance over the surface of the earth seemed complete.

However, there were still some features of the earth which remained a challenge to human exploration and at the top of this list was the highest point on the earth's surface – Mount Everest. As soon as in 1852, the Great Trigonometric Survey of India, declared Mount Everest to be the world's highest mountain, there was a surge of international interest in this peak belonging to the one of the youngest fold mountain ranges, the Himalayas. Foremost mountaineers from all countries became interested in climbing the summit which was now being seen as the ultimate geographic achievement.

The earliest attempts to climb Mt. Everest could begin only after 1921 after the hitherto reclusive mountain kingdom of Tibet opened its gates to people from other parts of the world. Among the many attempts to reach the summit, one of the most famous was the one including two British explorers George Mallory and Andrew Irvine. Mallory is known best for the iconic reply, "Because it's there", when asked the purpose behind attempting to climb the mighty peak and eventually it was to become the mantra for all enthusiasts of extreme adventure. However, Mallory's expedition was not to reach its destination and somewhere along the way, the two were believed to have got lost and died. In the next thirty years, there would be at least another ten expeditions attempting to reach the summit but all unsuccessful and ending in high human costs – these attempts would end in as many as thirteen climbers losing their lives.

Early Life

Edmund Hillary was born on July 20, 1919 in Auckland, New Zealand but grew up further south of the city at Tuakau, where his father had moved for farming. Ever since childhood thus Hillary was used to vast expanses of nature and this eventually developed into a fascination for mountaineering when, during a school trip, he climbed Mount Ruapehu, a well-known summit on the North Island of New Zealand. Upon completing high school, Hillary enrolled in the Auckland University where he studied maths and science.

Hillary's love of mountaineering soon drew him to the Southern Alps wherein 1939, he climbed 1933 metres to reach the summit of Mount Ollivier. Around this time, he decided to take up the seasonal job of a bee-keeper which would leave him free to pursue his first love of mountaineering, whether in his own country or in other ranges like the Alps of Europe.

The Himalayas of India and Nepal were fast becoming the new destination for all intrepid mountaineers across the world. As the world's youngest fold mountain range, this was home to some of the most formidable peaks on the planet, including the highest, Mount Everest. No wonder then Hillary found himself drawn to the Himalayas and within a short span of time, he had tamed around eleven peaks, all of which were over 20,000 feet or six thousand meters in altitude. The next logical target was naturally the highest of them all – Mount Everest.

Preparations to Climb Mount Everest

In 1951 and 1952, Hillary managed to find a berth in two expeditions that had been tasked to carry out surveys of mountain routes which could lead a team to Mount Everest. One of the fortunate results of his association with the surveying expeditions was that Hillary came into the notice of Sir John Hunt, who had been given the responsibility of leading an expedition sponsored by the Joint Himalayan Committee of the Alpine Club of Great Britain and the Royal Geographic Society in 1953. Hillary was thus made part of the 1953 expedition which set off for Mount Everest.

Mount Everest was known as a death trap for many reasons. Though it was not as technically difficult to climb it as K2 of the Karakoram range and the second highest peak on earth, the hazards of weather and terrain made Mount Everest a seemingly insurmountable destination. There were not only snowstorms, fierce winds with speed up to 125 mph and temperatures till minus 40 degrees Celsius to deal with, but unseen obstacles such as crevasses and sudden avalanches. Worst of all was the severe lack of oxygen which was as less as one-third as that of sea-level and which made the mountaineers vulnerable to nausea, headaches, blurred vision and even hallucinations as well as impaired co-ordination and judgment.

Hillary and his team thus spent months acclimatizing themselves to the icy climate and the lack of oxygen in the atmosphere. Usually, the mountaineers targeted Mount Everest in May or in October since at other times, the chances of bad weather were highest due to icy winters as well as monsoon storms.

Apart from the hazardous terrain and dangerous weather, the expedition also had to contend with the geopolitical forces. With the Chinese Government seizing control of Tibet, the North Pole route to Mount Everest was no longer accessible and thus the expedition had to change their plans and go by the South Pole route.

As the ascent became increasingly difficult, the climbers – overcome by exhaustion and lack of oxygen began dropping out one by one. In the end only two remained, Edmund Hillary and Sherpa Tenzing Norgay. At long last on May 29, 1953, the duo touched the summit of the world at 11:30 in the morning. The last frontier on the face of the earth had thus been conquered.

Hillary and Norgay spent around fifteen minutes at their hard-earned site on top of the world. And during this time Hillary took a photo of Norgay holding his ice axe strung with flags from Britain, India, Nepal and the United Nations. While Norgay, in keeping with his folk customs, dug a hole at the summit and buried sweets, Hillary preferred to leave behind a crucifix in the earth.

Other Expeditions

Hillary was feted by one and all, as the team returned to England. On the eve of Elizabeth II's coronation in June 1953, the conquest of Everest was announced to the world and as the first whiteman to have achieved it, Hillary was knighted by Queen Elizabeth II. He however was not the kind of person to rest on his laurels and soon turned his attention to other kinds of exploration, particularly that of the Antarctica. Between the years 1955 and 1958, Hillary was given the leadership of the New Zealand Chapter of the Commonwealth Trans-Antarctic Expedition. Also he was at the forefront of the first mechanized expedition to the South Pole that took place in 1958. Again during the Antarctic expedition of 1967, he was among the first to scale Mt. Herschel. He made other expeditions to the Everest region during the early 1960s but never again tried to climb to the top.

From the ice-bound land of the Antarctica, Hillary transported himself to the Himalayan Kingdom of Nepal in 1968 where he used a jet boat to travel the lengths of the fast flowing mountain rivers. Less than a decade later he landed in India in 1977, where he traced the course of the Ganges, from its mouth at Bay of Bengal to its origin in the glacier called Gangotri, that nestles high in the Himalayas.

However, not all was well in his personal life. In 1975, a plane carrying Sir Hillary's wife and daughter crashed and he was devastated by the loss of his family.

However, Sir Hillary soon rallied his physical and emotional strength and in 1985, he together with the first man to step on the surface of the moon, Neil Armstrong flew over the Arctic Ocean and even landed at the North Pole. This journey made Sir Hillary the first human being to visit both the North and South Poles as well as the highest point of earth, Mount Everest which came to be nicknamed the Third Pole.

Philanthropic Work

The regard that Sir Hillary's name commands around the world even today is not just because he was a great explorer and mountaineer – it is also because of his philanthropic work and his genuine concern for others' welfare, particularly the people of Nepal. During the 1960s, Sir Hillary spent several years in Nepal, helping to build hospitals, schools and airfields as well as identifying other areas of need. And best of all, he did it all without an iota of the whiteman's colonial condescension. In fact, Hillary wrote that he was proud that he and his team did not just stride into the Nepalese villages and tell the people what they needed: "We always responded to the wishes of the local people." In order to streamline his humanitarian work in Nepal, Sir Hillary established the Himalayan Trust which continues to formulate and execute projects aimed at bettering the lives of people living in the Himalayas.

As a measure of the great deal of goodwill his work created, he was chosen to serve as New Zealand's High Commissioner to Nepal, as well as India and Bangladesh, from 1985 to 1988. In recognition of his philanthropic work in Nepal and his sincere love for its people, Sir Hillary was awarded with the honorary Citizenship of Nepal in 2003 which also marked the 50th anniversary of conquering Mount Everest.

Sir Hillary was one of the earliest individuals to point out the threat of environmental degradation of the Himalayas. With mountain climbing becoming part of extreme adventure tourism and even serious expeditions multiplying in number, the slopes of the Himalayas became littered and strewn with junk. Eventually, Sir Hillary was able to convince the Government of Nepal to declare Mount Everest as a National Park which would put in place strict environmental safeguards.

Apart from leading a life of action and humanism, Sir Hillary was also a writer. In the 1955 book, *High Adventure*, he described the ascent to Mount Everest. His journey to the South Pole by tractor was the subject of two books, *The Crossing of Antarctica* published in 1958 which he co-wrote with Fuchs as well as *No Latitude for Error*, which was published in 1961. In 1975, Sir Hillary released his autobiography titled, *Nothing Venture, Nothing Win*.

His Legacy

At the age of 88 years, Sir Edmund Hillary died on January 11, 2008 after suffering from a heart attack. Because of his vast range of achievements, he was bestowed with numerous honours over the years. Apart from being knighted in 1953 by Queen Elizabeth II, he was awarded the *Order of the Garter* in 1995 by the same monarch. Again in 1987, Sir Hillary became a member of the 'Order of New Zealand' and was honoured with the Polar Medal for his participation in the Commonwealth Trans-Antarctic Expedition. In 1992, his home country, New Zealand issued a new five-dollar note that bore his image. Today several geographic landmarks bear Hillary's name, including a steep 12 metre rock wall on the Southeast ridge near Mount Everest peak which is now known as the Hillary Step. And though, *Time Magazine* listed him as one of the 100 most influential people of the 20th century, for many around the world, Sir Edmund Hillary simply remains, "New Zealand's most trusted individual".

□

19

Jacques Cousteau

(1910-1997)

With successful polar expeditions in the beginning of the 20th century as well as the ascent of Mount Everest or the Third Pole in the middle of the century, it seemed that the human mastery over the planet was complete. But while every bit of the surface of the earth had been indeed stamped with human presence, the oceans were an entirely different matter. It is here that the name of French naval officer and conservationist, Jacques Cousteau becomes important as he not only chartered new territory in the field marine exploration but encouraged people all over the world to appreciate the beauty of underwater world and work for its protection.

Early Life

On June 11, 1910, Jacques-Yves Cousteau was born in the village of Saint-André-de-Cubzac, in south-western France. His parents were Daniel and Elizabeth Cousteau and Jacques was the youngest of their two sons. As a child, Jacques struggled with health problems – he suffered from anaemia and was susceptible to stomach ailments. However, Jacques picked up swimming when aged only four and this marked a lifelong fascination with water and the world beneath its surface. At the same time, he began to grow interested in technology and when as an adolescent, he was presented with a movie camera, Jacques simply took it apart to see how it worked.

When he turned thirteen, Jacques was sent to boarding school in Alsace, France. Upon the completion of his preparatory studies, he enrolled in the Collège Stanislas in Paris. A defining step in his life was his entry to the Ecole Navale or the French Naval Academy at Brest, France in 1930, since this would provide the foundation for his future career in marine exploration.

Jacques Cousteau graduated from the Naval Academy as a gunnery officer but went onto join the French Navy's Information Service. This appointment took him to all the exotic islands and ports of the Indian and South Pacific Oceans where he took reels of photographs, both as part of his job and as a result of his own interest. In 1933, Cousteau was severely injured in an automobile accident and was advised to practice swimming to speed up his rehabilitation. At this time, he started swimming every day in the Mediterranean Sea and when a friend presented him with a pair of swimming goggles, Cousteau found an entirely new world under the water opening up before him. He found himself hooked to the mysteries of sea and its creatures and decided to extend his interest to the exploration of major oceans.

Personal Life

In 1937, Cousteau got married to a woman named Simone Melchior. The marriage resulted in two sons, Jean-Michel and Phillipe who would eventually follow Cousteau in the field of underwater expeditions. In 1990, Simone died and a year later, the aging explorer married Francine Triplet, with whom he had had a daughter and son earlier when he was still married to Simone.

The Initial Explorations

In order to escape the German occupation of Paris during the Second World War, Cousteau and his family lived in small town of Megreve, where France shared a border with Switzerland. At this time, Cousteau continued to experiment with the human ability to swim and explore under the water. In 1940, his efforts received a major boost when he made the acquaintance of Emil Gagnan, a

French engineer who was equally passionate about underwater explorations.

War Time Efforts

As the Second World War raged, a personality of Cousteau's stature could not remain out of action for long. He in fact joined the French Resistance Movement and began to track enemy troop movements as well as the actions of Italian soldiers who had joined forces with Germany. Even after the war came to an end, Cousteau worked with the French Navy to clear mines which had been laid deep into the seabed. However, between his missions, Cousteau continued to go on underwater expeditions, to explore, carry out experiments and sometimes to capture this mysterious world on film.

Invention of the Aqua Lung

One of the main requisites of underwater exploration was a device which would help the diver or swimmer easily breathe from oxygen. Fortunately, around this time came the invention of compressed air cylinders which fired Cousteau and Gagnan with even greater enthusiasm to design the right breathing apparatus and they started experimenting with snorkel hoses and body suits. The result of these efforts was the creation of the Aqua Lung which was made up of a valve-operated hose connecting the diver's mouth to a high-pressure cylinder worn on the back, thus making it possible for a diver to stay underwater for several hours.

The main advantage of this device was that it enabled divers to breathe underwater without an unwieldy diving suit. The Aqua Lung was first tested successfully in 1943 and it paved the way for underwater exploration as recreation and not just for scientific research. With the help of the Aqua Lung, for the first time any generally healthy person and not necessarily a professional diver could explore the underwater world of seas and oceans. Eventually, the Aqua Lung came to be modified and popularized as scuba gear with SCUBA being the acronym of Self-Contained Underwater Breathing Apparatus.

Deep Sea Exploration

For Cousteau and his colleagues, the Aqua Lung proved to be a crucial aid which enabled them to exploring and later film the depths of the seas and oceans that had never before been seen by human eye. One of the earliest underwater expeditions was in search of the ancient Roman shipwreck, Mahdia. In 1948, Cousteau together with his close aide Philippe Tailliez and other marine researchers as well as deep sea divers headed into the Mediterranean Sea to find remains of this Roman ship which was assumed to have sunk in around 80 BC. This exploration marked the beginning of underwater archaeology and was the also the first time that a large-scale expedition was making use of the Aqua Lung or self-contained diving apparatus that had been developed by Cousteau and his team.

Most of Cousteau's journeys out into the open seas took place in his ship named, Calypso which he leased in 1950. Under Cousteau's supervision, the Calypso was converted from a former British minesweeper to a research vessel fit for sailing long periods on oceans. Over time the Calypso became as much a part of the beloved image of the marine explorer as his iconic red beanie.

The success of Cousteau's book and award-winning movie, *The Silent World*, had held him to garner enough funds and attention. As a result in the 1950s, he set off on an underwater expedition that would explore the depths of the Red Sea and the Indian Ocean; this expedition was to be jointly sponsored by the French Government and the National Geographic Society.

In 1956, Cousteau led an expedition to explore the Romanche Trench, a deep depression in the Atlantic Ocean reaching to a depth of an incredible 25,354 feet. The crew set off on the Calypso, which later anchored with great difficulty like an angler's bobbin, on a 5½-mile nylon cable barely any thicker than a human finger. In the end the crew managed to anchor Calypso in 4½ miles of water – the deepest anchorage ever achieved by seafaring vessel at the time.

Later Cousteau and his crew photographed underwater life and the ocean floor of the Romanche Trench but even this posed its own challenges. Cousteau's photographer Edgerton, nicknamed "Papa Flash", by the crew of Calypso ensured that the camera was protected by a tempered stainless steel casing that could withstand the enormous pressure of the trench which would go up to as much as 5½ tons to the square inch.

Over the decades Cousteau continued to go on expeditions with the main purpose of revealing the mysteries of the deep to the world at large but eventually with also the intention of spreading awareness about the dangers of the destruction of marine habitats.

Underwater Habitat

Cousteau was also the force behind creation of the first underwater habitat for human beings. This kind of habitat could house humans within the ocean for weeks at a stretch. Though the United States Navy, was also working on something similar, Cousteau and his team were the first to get such an habitat functional.

The first underwater habitat pioneered by Cousteau and his team was Conshelf I, a steel cylinder, 5 meters long and 2.5 meters in diameter which was named Diogenes. In 1962, this was set up off the coast of Marseilles at ten meters depth. Two scientists named Albert Falco and Claude Wesly, were the first humans to live underwater in Conshelf I for a week.

In 1963, Cousteau and his team conceived Conshelf II, which was built on the floor of the Red Sea at a depth of ten meters depth. Five divers lived on Conshelf II for a month at the main house known as the "Starfish" while other parts of the habitat included aquarium, an equipment hangar and a garage for the diving saucer.

Conshelf III launched in 1965 off the coast of Nice was a much more ambitious project. This consisted of a building situated a hundred meters below the surface and which housed six oceanauts who would live together for three weeks.

The Conshelf series were launched with the purpose of understanding how living underwater over extended periods of time affected physiological and psychological traits of humans.

For one, the experiment proved that human beings could indeed live underwater but also that ultimately humans were not made to live in a world without the sun. Among other observations from the research project was that wounds healed faster in such a habitat while hair grew slower. The divers also discovered several new species of sea life and patterns of behaviour of sea creatures that had not been known before.

Environmental Activism

Cousteau had primarily started out as a marine explorer, seeking to plumb the hidden depths of the oceans and present its mysteries before the world in films and books. And for this purpose, in the beginning at least, he was not sentimental about marine creatures. In a gritty scene from *The Silent World*, the ship Calypso collides with a baby sperm whale. In order to spare the animal a lingering death, the crew kills it with a gunshot – and then incredibly even shoots the sharks that gather to feed on the now dead whale. At the time of re-editing during the 1990s there were concerns about letting such an apparently inhuman episode remain in the film but Cousteau was insistent that it should not be edited out – not only as a warning sign of what folly human beings are capable of but to show how far he had personally come down the path of environmental awareness.

Thus, it was only gradually that Cousteau's love for underwater exploration evolved into concern for the increasing degradation of marine habitats. But the main thing was that he felt a transformation and in keeping with that he began raising his voice against the widespread pollution of the seas and oceans as well as the destruction of underwater habitat.

One of the first steps of environmental activism that Cousteau took was in 1960 in which he strongly and publicly opposed a French-government plan to dump nuclear waste into the Mediterranean Sea. In fact he even took his fight straight to the President of the republic and insisted that General de Gualle himself look into the matter. Though Cousteau admitted that nuclear power had potential as a source of clean power but since nuclear waste is hazardous to the environment and there were still uncertainties about the correct form of its disposal, Cousteau believed that it should not be dumped in the oceans. The stand-off continued with women and children staged a sit-in on the tracks and ultimately environmentalists won the day as the train carrying the waste turned back.

Yet another aspect of his activism was devoted to the protection of whales against marine poachers and large-scale whalers. In fact, Cousteau worked tirelessly and where necessary personally appealed to the leaders of the northern countries to put an end to the practice of whaling. Partly as a result of Cousteau's unceasing efforts, in 1986. The International Whaling Commission, was finally able to get the number of votes necessary to pass the moratorium on commercial whaling.

His Films and Books

Part of the reason why Cousteau's underwater explorations were able to capture the imagination of people all over the world was their portrayal in films and books. Early on Cousteau realized the power of the media in generating interest as well as revenue for his expeditions. Among his earliest productions were two documentaries on underwater exploration, *Par dix-huit mètres de fond* or "18 Meters Deep" and *Épaves* or "Shipwrecks", made during the Second World War. In 1953, he published the immensely popular book, *The Silent World*, which was made into an Academy award-winning film in 1956. Then followed other films like, *The Golden Fish*, as well as *World Without Sun*, in 1966 which won an Academy Award as the best documentary feature of the year. For *The Silent World,* Cousteau collaborated with budding French film maker Louis Malle and so successful was this documentary about submarine exploration that it went on to win the prestigious Palme d'Or in 1956 for best picture at the Cannes Film Festival.

In 1966, Jacques Cousteau launched his first hour-long television show, "The World of Jacques-Yves Cousteau", on the ABC television network. In 1968, he produced the television series,

The Undersea World of Jacques Cousteau, whose popularity can be gauged from the fact that it ran for nine seasons.

After *The Silent World*, Cousteau wrote many other books, including a series titled *Undersea Discoveries of Jacques-Yves Cousteau.* Other than this, he wrote, *The Shark* in 1970, *Dolphins* in 1975, as well as *Jacques Cousteau: The Ocean World*, in 1985.

In 1973, Cousteau decided to put his growing celebrity status and increasing funding to good use and thus founded the Cousteau Society, an organization that is committed to spreading awareness of the ecosystems of the underwater world and the dangers that they face. Today, Cousteau Society is a well-known name in the world of underwater exploration and conservation besides boasting of more than 300,000 members from different parts of the globe.

Legacy

With more than 115 television films and 50 books on the subject of underwater exploration, Cousteau almost single-handedly brought the dark and fascinating world of deep oceans in the living room of viewers all over the world. He probably more than anyone was able to popularize the underwater mysteries as prime-time recreation and thus raise both interest and awareness for marine conservation issues too. A landmark event in deep sea exploration took place in 1960, U.S. Navy Lieutenant Don Walsh and Jacques Picard in the bathyscaphe, "Trieste", touched the bottom of the Mariana Trench which at 35,840 feet deep is the deepest point on the planet.

More specifically Cousteau had a big role to play behind the inventions of many deep sea equipment like the Aqua Lung and the special waterproof camera which could without the enormous pressure of deep sea exploration. Shortly after the invention of the Aqua Lung, dive shops in Europe and North America began supplying basic scuba diving equipment for recreational use. Apart from the Aqua Lung, Cousteau built a number of small piloted submersibles capable of shallow water dives. Such inventions have allowed divers and researchers to explore places once thought inaccessible to humans.

Also the idea behind the underwater habitat that Cousteau and his crew pioneered was eventually taken up by large-scale, industrial exploration since it was found that running an underwater habitat so that oceanauts could live and work there was ultimately economical than having them repeatedly lowered from ships for half an hour and then taken up again.

Over the course of his life, Jacques Cousteau was bestowed with many awards in recognition for his contribution to marine exploration and conservation. At the same time he was recognized for his resistance efforts during the Second World War, and awarded several medals, including the Legion of Honour, from his homeland France. The master underwater explorer and conservationist died unexpectedly in Paris on June 25, 1997, at the age of 87 years. □

20

Neil Armstrong

(1930-2012)

With mankind leaving their mark on the highest mountain peaks and plumbing the mysteries of the deepest oceans by mid-20th century, the only sphere left for further exploration was space. and this finally became a reality on April 12, 1961, when a 27-year-old Russian pilot named Yuri Gagarin made a single orbit of earth in a spacecraft called Vostok (East). This feat spurned USA, at that time the arch rival of USSR in space exploration, to hasten its efforts at sending the first manned mission to moon. And the man to take the iconic, "Small step for man, but a giant leap for mankind", was American space pilot, Neil Armstrong.

History of Space Exploration

Ever since the earliest humans began to understand their wider world, they have always been mystified by the sky and the objects like sun, moon and stars seen there. With growing scientific knowledge and technological advancement came the desire to conquer the skies and the world that lay beyond. The space age really began with the launch of the first artificial satellites in 1957 after which both the United States and the USSR were locked in a bitter fight to be the first to send a satellite to the Moon. On January 2, 1959 Luna-1 did become the first artificial object to escape Earth orbit and on September 14, the same year, Luna-2 became the first artificial object to strike the Moon.

The United States on the other hand had already began planning to sent manned mission to the moon which is why the next series of U.S. lunar probes, named Surveyor, was designed to, “soft-land” or land without crashing on the lunar surface and send back pictures. Even then the Soviets were able to achieve the first soft landing first, with Luna-9, on February 3, 1966. In response the United States launched the Lunar Orbiter probes, which began circling the Moon to map its surface in minute detail.

The race to the moon was now focused on piloted spaceflight since a human face carried a significance and identification that no artificial satellite or unmanned mission could on April 12, 1961, Yuri Gagarin became the first man to enter space while Alan Shepherd was the first American to do the same On May 5, 1961. Next year in February 1962 John Glenn became the first American to orbit Earth, logging five hours in space. By 1967 the United States and the USSR were each working on their spacecraft that was intended for lunar missions. The Soviets had created Soyuz while the Americans were developing Apollo. Each side continued to suffer some losses and victories in sending unmanned as well manned missions to the moon’s orbit. Finally, on July 16, 1969, the crew of the American Apollo 11—Neil Armstrong, Mike Collins, and Buzz Aldrin—headed for the Moon to attempt the lunar landing.

Early Life

Born on August 5, 1930 in Wapakoneta, Ohio, Neil Armstrong grew up to be a boy deeply fascinated with flying machines. He began taking flying lessons when he was just fifteen years of age and by next year had even earned his pilot’s license, way before he could be allowed to get a driver’s licence. In order to pursue his interest in aviation, Armstrong enrolled at the Purdue University with the intention of getting a degree in Aeronautical Engineering under the Holloway Plan.

So impressive was Armstrong’s performance at college that even before he finished his degree, he was selected by the Pensacola Naval Air Station in Florida in 1949 where he earned his wings at the age of twenty and thus became the youngest pilot in his squadron. Thereafter Armstrong was assigned to fly combat missions in Korea and here too he excelled, going onto win three medals, including the Korean Service Medal. But in keeping with the terms of the Holloway scholarship, Armstrong was sent home before the war ended so that he could complete his Bachelors degree. Later he completed his master's degree in Aeronautical Engineering from the University of Southern California in 1970.

Preparations for Space Flight

Armstrong was now eager to push new boundaries in aviation and thus decided to apply for the position of a test pilot with National Advisory Committee for Aeronautics which would later evolved into NASA. Though Armstrong was initially turned down, less than a year later he was called by NACA to report to their High Speed Flight Station at the Edwards Air Force Base in California. Here he logged in 2450 flying hours and signed up for test flights of more than 50 types of experimental aircraft. In the X-15 aircraft, Armstrong was able to achieve speeds of Mach 5.74 which is equal to 4,000 mph and reach an altitude of 63,198 meters or more than 207,500 feet.

In 1957, the Man on Space Soonest Program was launched in the United States and Armstrong's name was one of the first to figure in it. Around five years later, in September of 1963, Armstrong was again chosen as the first American civilian to enter space but was beaten by Russian woman Valentina Tereshkova who flew into space in June of 1963, thus becoming the first civilian in the world to do so.

However, Armstrong continued to be involved in other types of experimental spaceflights. In 1966, Armstrong flew on the Gemini 8 mission in which he was the Command Pilot. Again on Gemini 11, he served as the CAPCOM who is the main communicator with the astronauts when they are in space. By this time the Apollo series of lunar missions had been launched by the United States and Armstrong found himself appointed as the commander of the back-up crew of the Apollo 8.

Apollo 11 Mission

After years of preparation, finally On July 16, 1969, Apollo

11 left for the surface of the Moon with its crew of three astronauts – Neil Armstrong, Mike Collins and Edwin "Buzz" Aldrin. The launching site was Cape Canaveral, Florida on July 20, Apollo 11 arrived in orbit around the moon. After eight hours of preparation for the landing, the lunar module Eagle undocked from the command module Columbia and descended toward the Sea of Tranquillity.

Initially, Aldrin, as the Lunar Module Pilot, was deputed to be the one to exit the module and land on the moon. However, it was ultimately decided that since Armstrong was closer to the hatch, it would be easier for him rather than Aldrin to exit.

On July 20, 1969, Apollo 11 landed on the surface of the Moon whereupon Armstrong uttered the now famous words to mission control, "Houston, Tranquillity Base here. The Eagle has landed."

As Armstrong put down his left foot on the Moon's surface a defining moment in the history of human endeavour and space exploration was reached. Jubilation rang out through the Mission control at Houston and wonder settled upon billions of humans across the world. Mankind had now crossed the final frontier – that of space – and set foot on the Moon.

Fifteen minutes after Armstrong had exited the lunar module, Aldrin too joined him on the lunar surface. Then they planted the flag of the United States on the surface and left behind souvenirs in the memory of Soviet as well as American cosmonauts who had perished in the experimental stages of the lunar missions. As part of their scientific duties, they also collected around 22 kg of lunar rock samples and core tube samples. Additionally, they set up a solar wind experiment, a laser reflector and also a seismometer so as to detect moonquakes.

After spending around two and a half hours on the lunar surface, the astronauts then left back for the Earth and on July 24, 1969, their spacecraft landed in the Pacific Ocean. All the three astronauts who had been to Moon and back were felicitated by NASA and other global organizations as well as by President John Kennedy. Armstrong however was chosen to receive the highest civilian honour, the Presidential Medal of Freedom.

Later Years

After his service in Apollo 11, Armstrong did not take part in any other space mission though he continued his association with NASA in an administrative capacity and later joined the Defense Advanced Research Projects Agency as an adviser. Eventually, he found greater satisfaction in teaching and thus joined the University of Cincinnati as Faculty in the Department of Aerospace Engineering where he remained till 1979.

Because of his long experience with aerospace missions and considerable knowledge of space technology, Armstrong was requested to serve on investigative committees on two occasions – the first was set up after Apollo 13 accident while the second was convened to find out the reasons behind the Challenger explosion. In 1984, President Ronald Reagan appointed Armstrong to the National Commission on Space, an organization which was responsible for setting goals for the civilian space program into the 21st century.

Over the course of his later life, Armstrong served as a Director of several corporations and even hosted a 1991 television documentary on aviation which was titled, "First Flights." Till the end of his life, Armstrong continued to give his opinion NASA and current Space Policy. In one of the most recent statements that he made in the beginning of 2010, Armstrong roundly ticked off the plan of President Barack Obama to put an end to the Constellation Program.

On August 7, 2012, Armstrong was operated upon to relieve blocked coronary arteries. And even though, he seemed to responding well to the treatment, on August 25, Armstrong died due to surgery-associated complications. He was eighty-two years old.

Armstrong's first words after landing on the Moon continue to echo through time, long after that eventful day of July 1969; as his left foot stepped on the lunar surface, he said, "That's one small step for man, one giant leap for mankind." Today Armstrong is not only remembered for having fulfilled one of the oldest desires of humanity – that of landing on the moon – but that achievement paved the way for future space explorations, thus inspiring humans to cross the final frontier of the universe.

Looking Ahead

The 1960s had been marked by keen race the USA and USSR on who could notch up the most number of 'firsts' in space exploration. The next decade however saw a rare cooperative effort between the two superpowers as they came together for the first international manned spaceflight in history.

The mission was known as the Apollo-Soyuz Test Project under which NASA launched an Apollo spacecraft on July 20, 1975 which in turn joined a Soviet Soyuz in low-earth orbit. Over the course of next few days, astronauts of the ASTP performed several experiments to check the compatibility of docking systems of their respective spacecraft, the initiative also had a symbolic purpose. It not only marked the easing of a bitter space race between USA and USSR but paved the way for joint manned flights.

The next landmark in space exploration came in 1971 when the Soviets set up the first space station, Salyut 1. Now after a decade of human's first venture into space, they could live there for some time.

Ten years later another defining moment took place when NASA's space shuttle, Columbia, made its maiden flight and with it blasted off the first reusable space plane in the history of space exploration. Over the next three decades, the various shuttles continued to put in valuable work and a whopping total of 133 missions were launched in this time.

The beginning of the twenty-first century saw the International Space Station, taking shape in low-earth orbit; this was the result of the efforts of an international coalition of space agencies from major powers like USA, Japan, Canada and Europe. As the most expensive structure ever built by mankind, the ISS would help astronauts perform a variety of experiments in space, pursue exploration technology and develop knowledge for the well-being and superior performance of the crew out there.

It was only a matter of time before private players threw in their stake in this field and ushered in a new era of commercial space flights. In 2004, the manned, privately built SpaceShipOne made two round trips to suborbital space in the span of five days.

Again on December 8, 2010, Space Exploration Technologies, commonly known as SpaceX, became the first private company ever to launch a spacecraft to earth orbit and then recover it after re-entry. Virgin Galactic's VSS Enterprise vehicle is a sign of the times which announced plans of carrying paying customers on suborbital jaunts in around 2012, though each seat would come at a price of $200,000 upwards.

Thus, the history of human exploration has come a long way since the time, men looked up at the sky and wondered what was out there. The first explorations took place with mere survival as the aim as humans foraged for food and shelter to protect themselves from hostile environment. Over the centuries, mankind went on from strength to strength and with a mix of intelligence, perseverance and sheer daring, managed to bring every part of the earth, down from the deepest oceans to highest mountain peak within the ambit of human knowledge. And now human beings are ready to blast into space not just as researchers but as tourists too.

And yet the nature of creation being what it is, mankind is constantly discovering new facts about the universe. Certain places on earth like Papua New Guinea and Darien Gap in Western Hemisphere continue to entice explorers with their wealth of undiscovered plant and animal life while others like northeast Greenland have some peaks which have not even been named. Then there is sub-glacial Antarctica where the intricate network of waterways could contain hitherto-unknown forms of life.

And even though most of the Moon's surface has been mapped, vast stretches still remain unexplored like the lunar South Pole, some features of which have been thought to be ideal to contain frozen water. Likewise, a manned mission to Mars would be another event to look forward to since the Red Planet has inspired hundreds of theories of life outside earth.

All these are only some of the challenges that remain for future intrepid explorers to take up.

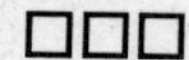